AFTER MIDNIGHT
Allan Leverone

1

The man finished tidying up his basement workshop and smiled, pleased with himself. A place for everything, and everything in its place.

Cleaning the workshop had been a simple task, since virtually nothing was out of place to begin with. Still, knowing his tools were all stored exactly where he wanted them gave the man peace of mind; a sense of accomplishment that he had to admit had little to do with actually accomplishing anything.

He glanced around the basement. Small hand tools—hammers, wrenches and the like—hung neatly from a gigantic pegboard bolted onto one basement wall, while larger power tools such as his belt sander and electric jigsaw were tucked away in specially constructed bins stacked neatly under his workbench. The basement floor had been swept and then swept again until the man felt confident he could eat off the concrete if he wanted to.

He nodded in satisfaction. The man's impressive housekeeping skills were rarely put to use in the rest of the house, and the irony of this fact did not escape him. His wife called him "The Human Hurricane," most of the time fondly, for his consistently demonstrated propensity for messing up a room within minutes of stepping foot in it.

But the rest of the house was different. That was Gina's territory. The basement workshop was *his*. His wife rarely ventured down here, and when she did, it was only to express the obligatory admiration for one of his woodworking creations before retreating within minutes to her own sanctuary upstairs.

After one last look around—everything was still shipshape; nothing had defied the laws of physics by moving itself—the man walked briskly to the stairs and began climbing. He had told Gina he would watch a movie with her tonight, some sci-fi thing about a young girl who had to shoot flaming arrows at people in order to survive. Or something.

It didn't sound like the man's cup of tea, but even after all these years he loved Gina and wanted her to be happy. He preferred gritty crime dramas to fanciful accounts of futuristic worlds, or sparkly vampires, or whatever was currently in vogue, but he had been married plenty long enough to recognize the truth of the old adage, "Happy wife, Happy life."

He would watch the movie.

Halfway up the stairs, and apropos of absolutely nothing, the man had a sudden thought. It came out of nowhere and arrived fully formed in his brain: he needed to sharpen his letter opener.

It was a ridiculous notion, at least in part because the letter opener would be at work, not here at home. Work was where he used it. He could picture its location perfectly, because he always kept the opener in exactly the same place: right side of his desk inside a little wooden basket Gina had given him years ago. In addition to the letter opener, the basket contained a multitude of pens, pencils and markers.

He shook his head and climbed one more step and then another thought struck him, again coming out of nowhere like a bolt of lightning and again fully formed. He should reach into the left front pocket of his pants.

He did so immediately, almost out of instinct, virtually no conscious thought involved. He blinked in surprise as his fingers closed around a metallic object with a short handle and long, dull blade tapering to a blunt-edged tip.

His letter opener.

The man withdrew it from his pocket and stared at it in slack-jawed wonder. Why the *hell* would he have brought the damn thing home?

To sharpen it, of course.

Ah.

To sharpen it. Of course.

But why now? Why was it so important to sharpen a fifty-year-old gold-plated commemorative letter opener when he had never once had occasion to do so in the entire time he had owned it?

And more to the point, how had it ended up in the man's pocket? He must have put it there, undoubtedly in anticipation of sharpening it in his workshop tonight, but for the life of him, the man could not recall having done so. It was the sort of thing he should remember.

He stood motionless, halfway up the basement stairs, his movie night with Gina forgotten. It was critical he sharpen this important office tool; that was what he needed to keep foremost in his mind. The fact that he could not recall bringing the letter opener home was mildly interesting but ultimately irrelevant.

The man turned and retreated down the stairs, stepping with a sense of urgency to his workbench. He opened one of the drawers beneath it, removed a pair of plastic goggles and placed them on his face. He then opened a second drawer and pulled out a pair of work gloves, sliding his hands into them.

Next, he turned to his left, where an electric grinding wheel had been bolted to the wooden table. He lowered a reinforced glass shield mounted on a flexible arm until it hung suspended over the wheel.

He flipped a power switch and the grinding wheel powered up with a smooth *whir*. Within a second it was spinning at full RPMs, and the man carefully lowered the letter opener to the wheel, holding it firmly in both hands.

Tiny sparks began to shower off the surface. It looked like an ant-sized Fourth of July fireworks display. The man eased the length of the letter opener's blade along the spinning wheel, then turned it over and repeated the process, paying careful attention to the tip. It was important the tip be honed to a razor-sharp point.

A moment later he was done. He flipped the power switch off and the grinding wheel whirred to a stop. The man slipped off his gloves and removed his goggles, being careful to replace each item in its appropriate drawer.

Then he examined the result of his labor.

It looked good; a fact that surprised the man not at all. He was an experienced woodworker/home repairer and when he started a job, he expected to complete it to his own high standards.

He had done exactly that.

The man slipped the letter opener back into his pocket, handling the little tool much more carefully now than he had a few moments ago. It was suddenly considerably more dangerous.

His work complete, the man returned to the stairs and began climbing, once again ready for his movie night with Gina. His previous unease regarding the letter opener and why he had removed it from his office was forgotten.

What difference did it make, anyway?

2

Mack Pender liked to think of himself as an administrator. A businessman. As the top law enforcement official at Bridgewater State Hospital, home to those Massachusetts inmates determined by an impartial justice system to be criminally insane, he couldn't kid himself, though.

He was a prison warden.

Still, despite the fact that his biweekly paychecks arrived courtesy of the Massachusetts Department of Corrections, "administrator" seemed a much more civilized title. To Mack, the term "warden" evoked images of 1930s black-and-white gangster films, of James Cagney talking tough and overacting inside Hollywood's romanticized notion of prisons after shooting up the insides of banks with his tommy gun. The title just seemed dated.

And after nearly three decades on the job, the last half of which had been spent right here in the corner office at Bridgewater, Mack felt he had earned the right to picture himself however the hell he wanted.

As administrator, he had always felt it was critical his employees understand that they had the support of management, particularly in a high-stress environment like Bridgewater State Hospital. The fact that the residents of this facility were considered in the eyes of the law to be irresponsible for their own criminal actions—incapable of understanding right from wrong—made them *more* dangerous than typical inmates, not less.

One of the first things Mack had done after inheriting the administrator's job back in 2000 was to sit down with every single staff member, one on one, and emphasize to them that his door was always open. He had done the same thing with all employees hired in the intervening years and intended to continue doing so as long as he was in charge.

The fact of the matter was, though, that Mack Pender's open-door policy had yielded little in the way of actual visits from his staff over the last fifteen years. Prison guards—and that's what they were, guards, no matter how big the Massachusetts Department of Corrections spelled out Hospital on the sign at the front gate—were first and foremost a part of the law enforcement community. And that community valued chain of command more than almost anything else. Prison guards simply weren't wired to go to the Big Boss with their complaints.

Still, Mack Pender wasn't one to be easily dissuaded from something he believed in. The open-door policy had been one of the keystones of his administration, and he applied it literally. Rarely was his office door closed.

Today, though, as he parked his car and strolled toward the front entrance of Bridgewater State Hospital, it occurred to Mack that it might be a good idea to suspend his open-door policy, just for a little while. *I have business that needs to be conducted in private.*

He stopped a moment, confused, wondering where the hell *that* thought had come from. There wasn't a single bit of business he needed to conduct privately, today or most other days.

After a moment, Mack resumed walking, shaking his head. Maybe he was overtired. Maybe it was time to get away. Gina had been bugging him to take a vacation; he hadn't done so in years. Perhaps now was the time.

When he reached the door, Mack smiled warmly and nodded to the guard, intending to pause for a couple of minutes and pass the time of day with him. Then everything changed. For the second time in a matter of seconds, the warden halted in his tracks and shook his head, blinking in confusion.

He felt funny.

Not ill, exactly, just funny. Strange.

It made Mack forget all about the meaningless conversation he had intended to share with Officer Tommy Bradbury. Suddenly it became very important he get to his office. Close the door. Do something that at first blush shocked the hell out of him but after a moment's reflection seemed utterly logical. Necessary, even.

Mack realized Tommy was talking to him, had been for several seconds now. He was saying something about the Patriots' stupid offseason personnel moves: "...and they call Belichick a genius? Man, without Mayo that defense just isn't up to par. It's gonna be a long season if they can't shut down the opposing quarterbacks."

"Yeah, defense," Mack agreed. "It's the key to building a championship team."

He didn't give a damn about the New England Patriots, hadn't watched an entire game from beginning to end in at least ten years. But it seemed that the local teams were a subject of unrelenting importance to most of his staff, so Mack had always made an effort to keep up, at least enough to speak with his people semi-intelligently on the subject of sports.

Not now, though. Now he had important duties to attend to. He noted Bradbury's surprise at the fact he had resumed walking. Noted it but didn't care.

"We'll get 'em next week," he said to Tommy as he passed, too distracted to consider the fact that it was February and the Patriots' season wouldn't begin for another six months.

Tommy wrinkled his forehead in surprise but said nothing. Mack was glad. He could tell from Tommy's response that he had said something wrong, but had wasted far too much time here at the front door already when he had time-critical business to take care of in his office.

Once inside the prison/hospital complex, Mack picked up his pace. For the life of him, he couldn't remember what was so important he had to get started right away, but he knew it was a top priority and needed to be knocked out immediately.

He hit the outer office almost at a dead run, shoving the wooden door open without stopping. Without even slowing. It swung violently inward and nearly decapitated Mack's longtime secretary, Nancy Bickford. The elderly lady was bent at the waist, leaning over a large filing cabinet that had been placed inopportunely next to the door. She managed to pull her head back just in the nick of time.

The rush of displaced air ruffled Nancy's hair, giving her a rumpled appearance, which Mack barely noticed. It caused her also to glare severely at her boss, which Mack *did* notice.

He skidded to a stop with a distracted smile. "I'm sorry, Nancy, I had no idea you were right there. I hope I didn't startle you."

"Startle, yes. Injure, no. Fortunately. What's your hurry? It's not even eight a.m."

Mack still could not remember why he was in such a rush to start the day. After a moment, he realized Nancy was gazing frankly at him, awaiting a response. It was like being a teenager forty years ago, dealing with his mother after getting caught red-handed with an unsmoked joint in his underwear drawer.

Finally he said, "Uh, just a busy day ahead of me, I guess. A lot to do. You know how it is."

She continued to stare at him, eyebrows raised. The implication was clear: *you've lost your mind and no amount of searching is going to get it back.*

Instead of saying that, though, Nancy Bickford just shook her head and said, "All right, Tiger, go get 'em. Just slow down, so you don't kill me in the process." Then she barked out a laugh and bent back over the filing cabinet.

Mack continued into his office, closing the door behind him, officially and irrevocably—for now—nullifying his open-door policy. He took two steps into the room before returning to the door and locking the knob. *Today's work is important. Mustn't be disturbed.*

He moved to the reinforced glass window looking out into Nancy's antechamber and tugged on the little-used string to lower a set of cheap plastic blinds. As they fell, he observed Nancy Bickford looking up in surprise. He locked eyes with her for a half second and then Mack twisted the plastic wand hanging off the right edge of the blinds, levering them closed and ensuring his privacy.

He sighed in satisfaction and glanced around the room, anxious to get started.

He walked to his desk and sat behind it in his well-worn leather executive's chair.

He then examined the clutter, not sure what he was looking for, but confident he would know it when he saw it.

There was a stack of paperwork roughly two inches high; a weekend's worth of daily status reports on all inmates. Mack shook his head. These would have to be reviewed and signed off on at some point this morning, but they weren't of a critical nature. They could wait.

There was an equipment requisition: for a television to replace the one in the guards' break room that had finally burned out after twenty-some years. That could wait, too.

There was Mack's desktop computer, which he powered on. It started whirring and clicking as it booted up.

There was an inbox and an outbox, filled with assorted evidence of the bureaucracy without which government enterprise could not possibly operate.

There was a stack of official correspondence, for some reason placed next to instead of inside the inbox, which up until quitting time yesterday had been held down by a gold letter opener with the words "1855–Bridgewater State Hospital–1955" stamped along both sides of the blade. The opener had been a commemorative item celebrating the prison/hospital's one-hundredth anniversary and had been passed on to Mack by the previous warden, who had inherited it from *his* predecessor.

There was a—

Wait a minute.

Mack looked at the stack of correspondence. He reached into his pocket and removed the letter opener that had so recently sat atop the stack of papers, the one that had been so important that he sharpened it last night at home.

He placed it on his desk and examined it with interest.

The thing was in remarkably good condition for being a half-century old; certainly it had held up to the passage of time better than the facility for which it had been issued. Despite being in a near-constant state of remodeling, Bridgewater's best days were well behind it, if they had ever existed at all.

Mack picked up the opener and ran his index finger along the cutting edge. Poked the tip. It wasn't exactly razor-sharp, but it just might do.

He dropped it onto the surface of his desk with a clatter at the same time a brief knock came at his office door. "Warden Pender? Sir? Is everything all right?"

It was Nancy. Mack worked to control his impatience. He should have expected this. Nancy Bickford was an outstanding secretary: prompt, courteous and organized to a T. The office, and indeed, to a large extent the entire facility, ran as smoothly as it did thanks to her efforts.

And the reason things ran so smoothly was because Nancy was a creature of habit. Stern and forbidding in many ways, she was like an iron-fisted schoolteacher. So this departure from the norm—Mack's closing and locking his office door—had thrown Nancy for a loop.

"Yes, Nancy, everything's fine." Mack raised his voice so it would carry through the closed door, doing his best to keep the impatience out of his voice. "It's just that I really need to buckle down and get this project done."

"Oh. All right. I'll leave you alone then." Nancy sounded hesitant. It was clear she was uncomfortable with this disruption in the usual routine and wasn't sure how to proceed. "You'll let me know if you need anything." She phrased it as a statement.

"Of course. And don't worry, this won't take long."

Mack waited a moment and when there was no further interruption, he returned his attention to the commemorative letter opener glittering in gold on the surface of his desk.

He considered whether it would serve his purposes.

Couldn't decide.

Undoubtedly there was a pair of scissors around somewhere, probably under lock and key inside a drawer in Nancy's desk. Given the nature of Bridgewater State Hospital's mission, it would be career suicide to leave scissors where there was even a chance they could be accessed by the wrong people. In fact, strictly speaking, the letter opener shouldn't have been out in the open, either. But he had always used the damned thing, and there had never been a problem. Besides, he was the boss; who the hell would anyone complain to?

He considered calling Nancy on the intercom and asking her about scissors, even picked up the phone and prepared to buzz her.

Then he changed his mind. Hung up the phone. Given his secretary's already-expressed concern, he felt that asking her to dig up a pair of scissors would only lead inevitably to more questions, more expressions of concern, and more hassles he didn't need.

He picked up the letter opener again and ran his left index finger along the cutting edge as he had done a moment ago, only this time Mack pressed firmly. A narrow gash opened up in his finger as the tool sliced deep into the tender flesh.

Mack gasped quietly. He was determined not to upset Nancy, whom he pictured listening just on the other side of the door. A river of bright red blood welled up inside the furrow he had opened, overflowing its banks a moment later and running down the length of his finger. The blood began dripping onto the surface of his desk, spattering in a delicate pattern on his blotter/desk calendar.

He had cut himself badly.

He smiled. The letter opener would work just fine.

Mack leaned over his desk, concentrating hard, staring at the office tool as he tried to determine the most efficient way to accomplish his task. He was anxious to get started, but a lifetime of career experience had taught him the importance of thorough planning. A task worth doing was worth doing right.

He gripped the opener in his right hand and then his left, lifting it and picturing in his mind what he needed to accomplish. The blood continued to drip onto his desk, now flowing more steadily. Mack thought there should be some serious pain from the deep gash, but he barely felt any. He prided himself on his ability to focus, to devote his full attention on what was important.

Finally he decided on the most efficient course of action. It would involve holding the opener in his left hand, the one that was now bleeding profusely. He wished he had used a finger of his right hand to test the blade, but hadn't thought things through before doing so, and now would have to adjust.

Hopefully the blood leaking out of his finger wouldn't cause his grip to slip when he needed it most.

Mack moved everything out of the way, doing his best to avoid splashing too much blood around. The daily inmate status reports and stack of correspondence he placed in two neat piles on the carpeting next to his desk. The equipment requisition went into his inbox. He left his computer running.

Preparations complete, Mack pulled his chair up close to the desktop, sliding it forward until his ample belly pressed tightly against the surface. He lifted his head as if staring at something on the ceiling and stretched his neck taut.

He gripped the letter opener as firmly as he could in his left hand, making a fist and wrapping his fingers around the haft, with the blade protruding out the small gap between his thumb and bleeding forefinger, using the thick pad of skin in the webbing for support.

He placed his elbow on the top of his desk and extended his arm across his body until his fist was suspended several inches to the right of his neck.

He took a deep breath and smiled. This was going to be easy.

Mack wrapped his right hand around his left for a little extra support and punched the letter opener through the skin of his neck, burying it as deeply into his throat as possible.

Blood spurted from the puncture wound and mixed with what was already flowing from the gash in his finger, dripping down the side of his neck and under the collar of his shirt. As with the cut on his finger, Mack knew he should be experiencing extreme pain, but all he could feel was a bit of minor discomfort.

He took a breath and was amused to hear a gurgling sound coming from the small hole in the right side of his neck. Mack chuckled and began sawing steadily, forcing the letter opener through muscle and gristle, working it right to left across his throat.

The flow of blood increased significantly as the wound became larger.

Black spots began to blossom in Mack's vision.

He worked harder, determined to complete the morning's most important task.

He groaned and then went silent as the letter opener severed the muscles of his Adam's apple.

Mack Pender's last thought before losing consciousness and toppling onto his blood-soaked desk was that he had done a damned fine job. He had almost—not quite, mind you, but almost—managed to slit his own throat from ear to ear.

3

C aitlyn Connelly sipped a glass of wine and smiled at her boyfriend. Kevin Dalton's injuries were healing nicely and he seemed to be suffering few lingering effects from nearly being killed last year in a tiny Revere, Massachusetts house at the hands of a madman.

Cait wished she could say the same about herself. Physically, she was doing okay, she supposed. The surgeons said the skin grafted onto her arm where Milo Cain had begun peeling it like an apple was healing well. There had been no significant issues with infection and the pain was manageable.

Yes, physically she was recovering, if slowly.

Mentally was a different story.

Getting a full night's rest had become a thing of the past, a fantasy, an elusive and unreachable goal. Falling asleep was difficult, staying asleep impossible. It didn't matter how exhausted she was or how late she stayed up. She tried working out late in the day, jogging long distances, taking sleeping pills, all in an effort to knock herself out so badly she could just sleep.

Nothing worked. Every evening was the same: a monumental struggle to drop off, sleep coming only with the utmost reluctance, hours of tossing and turning, kicking off the blankets, pulling up the blankets, lying on her side, on her belly, on her back. Finally falling asleep, only to be tortured by the nightmares.

And they were always the same. Always.

In her nightmares, Cait found herself strapped to a couch, naked and afraid, as a shadowy man, faceless but for a leering mouth, came at her with a razor-sharp carving knife. The man would hold the knife in front of her eyes, turning it this way and that, explaining with utter lack of emotion what he was going to do to her. How he was going to slice her, stab her, impale her on the blade's end.

Then he would begin. He would peel the skin away from her arm, reveling in her screams, the pain fiery and unrelenting. He would move to her face, and start slicing the skin, row after row, hairline to jaw, until there was nothing left but a grinning skull where her face once was, the pain enormous, Cait wishing she could die just to escape it, and then—

And then she would awaken, moaning and crying, sometimes screaming softly, sometimes reduced by the magnitude of the imagined pain to gasping silence, drenched in sweat, the bedcovers twisted around her writhing body, Kevin, blessed Kevin, deep sleeper that he was, snoring softly away beside her.

Cait forced herself away from her thoughts and back to the present. The waiter had taken their dinner order and was walking away. Cait noticed Kevin gazing at her appraisingly. He had been doing that a lot lately.

"What?" she said defensively.

"Where were you?"

She shrugged. "The usual."

"You look like hell," he said softly.

She chuckled. "Thanks. You really know how to sweet-talk a girl."

"You know what I mean. The dreams aren't getting any better, are they?"

She shrugged again. She had never confessed to anyone—not even to Kevin—just how horrifying her nightmares were, or how reliably consistent. But he would have had to be utterly oblivious not to notice her distress, no matter how deep a sleeper he was. And Kevin Dalton was *not* oblivious.

She glanced into his piercing blue eyes and then looked away. Sometimes holding his intense gaze was too difficult, especially when it seemed he could see right into the core of her being. "I think I just need some time."

"Time? It's been months, Cait, and I know for a fact you're not sleeping any better now than you were right after...it...happened."

She had no answer for that. What could she say? He was right.

He lifted the wineglass to his lips and then placed it back on the table without drinking. "I think you should see someone. You know, just to talk."

This again.

They had had this conversation many times, and while Cait could not argue the point—there was no question he was right; she was at least self-aware enough to recognize that fact—she just couldn't bring herself to discuss with anyone the main issue: that her own brother had tried to murder her, and in the most gruesome manner possible.

"I'm not ready," she said quickly, reflexively.

Kevin shook his head slightly, not able to hide his disappointment. "Maybe you're going to have to do it *before* you're ready. Maybe you'll never *be* ready until you kick yourself in that cute little ass of yours and just do it."

Cait smiled. "It always comes down to my ass with you, doesn't it?"

"Of course. Your ass is the eighth wonder of the world. And don't change the subject."

Cait wanted nothing more than to change the subject, but the problem with dating a cop was that he was like a bulldog once he clamped onto something. He was relentless. It was a personality trait that had damned near gotten him killed last summer.

"I'll think about it," she mumbled, knowing she would do no such thing and suspecting strongly he knew it as well.

"What about you?" she asked. "How in the world are you able to sleep like a baby after what happened?"

"What makes you think I sleep like a baby?"

"I'm right next to you when you do it, remember? And I'm up most of the night, while you snore away, lost in a peaceful slumber."

Kevin laughed. "Okay, you got me. I do sleep pretty well, now that you mention it."

Cait spread her arms. "How? I thought you were dead that day inside my mother's house. How do you not relive it over and over in your head?"

"I guess it comes down to my job. When you're a cop, you only rarely see the best in people. Most of the time you're confronted with the ugliest behavior human beings are capable of inflicting on each other. Now, Milo Cain was a whole different brand of evil, I'll grant you that, but I think I've been inoculated against some of the worst effects of that kind of evil after seeing it day after day. Kind of like a flu shot, maybe."

Now it was his turn to shrug. "If I couldn't compartmentalize, I think I would have been forced to find a new line of work years ago." He looked at her sadly. "Believe me, baby, if I could take away your pain, I would do it in a heartbeat."

"I know," Cait said. But she wouldn't wish the endless sleepless nights on her worst enemy. Up until a few months ago, Caitlyn Connelly would have scoffed at the notion of even *having* a worst enemy. She had been a more-or-less anonymous thirty-year-old real estate lawyer, successful in her career and without a single enemy in the world. Or so she had thought.

Now she recognized the foolishness of that belief.

She knew who her worst enemy was, all right.

But how could she wish ill will on her own brother?

4

Milo Cain lay in his hospital bed listening to the conversation of people who had not the slightest inkling he could hear them. Today it was two nurses, here for their semi-regular attempt at providing him care. Changing his bedsheets. Giving him a sponge bath and then dressing him in fresh pajamas. Cleaning his small hospital room/ prison cell. Replacing his nearly full colostomy bag with an empty one.

Milo didn't give a damn about any of that.

What he *did* give a damn about, however, was their conversation. The nurses were yakking with the unrestrained enthusiasm of gossipers who had latched onto one of the juiciest stories ever and were determined to rehash it for days on end and from all possible angles. They weren't just going to beat the dead horse; they intended to pound it over and over until the corpse was nothing more than an unrecognizable bloody pulp.

If he had been capable of feeling emotion, Milo might actually have liked these girls.

He listened closely. It was easy enough to do, and not just because he was comatose and paralyzed from the neck down. The nurses didn't seem the least bit concerned about discretion or lowering their voices. Milo pictured other employees walking past in the prison hospital hallway, hearing the conversation coming from the coma patient's room and shaking their heads in disgust. He smiled inside.

"Did you hear how they found him?" Milo pictured this nurse as blonde and petite, slim but not skinny. Big tits.

"He was locked in his office, wasn't he?" This one he guessed to be a little older, maybe slightly overweight. Pleasingly plump but not grossly corpulent. The thicker the cushion, the better the pushin', and all that. She would have dark hair and would wear it in a ponytail.

"Yes! He locked himself in his office and tried to saw his own freaking head off with a letter opener, do you believe that?"

The second nurse made appropriate noises of disgust but then said, "I heard there was a lot of blood." Milo thought he could sense a trace of excitement in her voice. A good girl discussing naughty things.

"A lot of blood? Of *course* there was a lot of blood, he slit his throat practically from ear to ear! I heard it was all over his desk, like a little mini ocean or something. I heard there was so much blood it soaked into the carpet and the whole thing will have to be replaced."

"His secretary saw it all, didn't she?"

"Well, she was there, but he locked his office door, remember? So I don't think she actually *saw* anything. I heard she banged on the door for like fifteen minutes after he offed himself before she finally called for help. When they forced his door open, I heard she screamed so loud you could hear her throughout the whole damned complex!"

Not true, Milo thought. *I was listening closely and I heard nothing.* He had to give the young nurse points for imagination and enthusiasm, though.

Now the second nurse lowered her voice, as if suddenly realizing the subject was taboo, that maybe it wasn't the smartest career move to discuss the suicide of your boss with such obvious glee. "I wonder how long it took him to die."

"Couldn't have been long," the slim blonde nurse said confidently. "There was so much blood he wouldn't have been able to last more than a couple of minutes before dropping onto his desk like a rag doll."

"Why do you suppose he did it? And in such a...horrible...way?"

Milo could almost see the first nurse shrug. "Who knows? He obviously had mental problems, but the funny thing is that his wife and secretary both claim he was acting completely normal that morning, right up to the time he locked his door and started slicing his throat like he was carving up a Thanksgiving turkey."

"Well, he obviously wasn't normal."

"Obviously. But how could anyone even *act* like everything was fine when their intention was to cut their own head off in the next few minutes?"

The conversation continued, the nurses beating the dead horse—and warden—to their hearts' content, but Milo tuned them out. He had learned all he needed to know. His experiment had been successful beyond his wildest dreams.

He had thought his life was over after failing in his quest to rid the world of that self-righteous little bitch Caitlyn Connelly, the young woman who had turned out to be his twin sister and who had benefitted from every advantage the world had to offer, while *he* had been forced to suffer through life, tortured by visions and compulsions no one would ever understand and the knowledge he would never be normal.

Getting shot in the face by the little bitch wasn't bad enough; losing an eye to a hunk of lead fired from point-blank range wasn't bad enough. He had had the extreme misfortune to break two vertebrae in his back when he fell. Now he was not just a comatose freak but a paralyzed one as well.

But Milo's attitude reversed itself by one hundred eighty degrees not long after his arrival here at Bridgewater, his permanent home. He had discovered, purely by accident, that his ability to "see" things in his head, the random snatches of people's lives known as "Flickers" by his bitch-sister, had not disappeared when he was attacked.

In fact, just the opposite was true. He discovered that now, in addition to seeing those random snatches of people's lives, he had somehow developed the unexpected and heretofore unimagined ability to *influ-*

ence those people, to *push* thoughts and ideas—suggestions—into their heads.

Why that would be the case, Milo Cain had not the slightest notion. Presumably, the two slugs he had taken to the head from point-blank range had scrambled the circuitry of his brain enough to slightly alter the ability he had always possessed. The ability he had considered the worst kind of curse for most of his life.

Thanks to his paralysis and his comatose state, Milo had had plenty of time to dwell on the bizarre occurrence, and the theory about his brain circuitry becoming inadvertently rewired was the best he could come up with. Ultimately, though, it didn't matter why he could do the things he was now capable of.

What mattered was that he could do them.

And now, despite being stuck inside a broken and unsalvageable body, permanently lost and alone, trapped in a situation most people would consider the worst form of inhuman torture, Milo had never been happier. Had never felt more alive.

Because the fact of the matter was that life as he had been living it before, homeless and on the streets, huddled inside an abandoned Boston tenement building with no heat, with hookers, pimps and drug dealers everywhere, had in many ways been its own form of torture.

He had done his best to make life livable by playing his little games, haunting the city, plucking the most vulnerable of the young prostitutes off the streets and making them his pets, torturing them with his knives, scalpels, pliers and other tools, piercing their skin and peeling their flesh, but he realized now how much he had been at risk.

Through his advanced intelligence and a little luck, he had managed to stay one step ahead of the law—at least until the disastrous run-in with the evil bitch in Revere—but looking back at his situation now, with the benefit of time and perspective, Milo knew his fate had always been sealed. Sooner or later his games were bound to end. He had been killing time, in addition to young girls.

But not now.

Now, everything was different.

Now, Milo Cain held the power. It was hilarious, a cosmic joke of the utmost magnitude. From here, helpless and alone in a hospital bed—and not just any hospital bed, a *prison* hospital bed—Milo could now wreak havoc and destroy the lives of all the people he wanted to, whenever he wanted to.

And who was going to stop him? Hell, who would even *suspect* him: a comatose patient, unable to move or even communicate, unfeeling and unaware as far as the medical community was concerned? It would never happen. Milo was finally free to pursue his wildest fantasies with impunity, no matter how gruesome the crime or how large the pool of potential victims.

This was what he took from the inane conversation of the two ditzy nurses cleaning him and his room.

Because Mack Pender had been an experiment.

His experiment.

He had *pushed* the suggestion of suicide into Pender's brain as the warden prepared for work a couple of mornings ago. Milo had laid out the plan, step by step, being very specific, to see just how far he could go. Whether the power had limits.

Was it a form of hypnosis? Supposedly, no one could be made to do anything under hypnosis they would not do when fully aware. No one could be hypnotized to murder his neighbor or rape his cousin, or so the theory went. Milo had never been sure he believed that, but in the past the issue had always been a theoretical one, had never really mattered because it had not applied to him.

Now it did matter. Greatly. Now he needed to experiment. To test his limits. So he had pushed the suggestion into Pender's head, specifying the most violent and gruesome method of self-execution he could conceive while also satisfying his predilection for knives and sharp-edged instruments.

And it had worked beautifully. Pender, who as far as Milo knew was a normal (ha!), well-adjusted family man, not suicidal or self-destructive in any way, had slipped under Milo Cain's spell, not resisting his task in the slightest.

Pender had been miles away at the time the suggestion was implanted, too, telling Milo that physical proximity was not necessary for successful implantation of a suggestion.

This knowledge was critical.

Because Milo had plans. Lots of them.

But before he could begin implementing those plans, he needed to think. And to think, he needed quiet. And since he wasn't capable of getting up and walking away, it was now time to drive those two chattering magpies out of earshot.

Without much effort, Milo *pushed* a suggestion into the head of the first nurse, the younger one with the slim build and the blonde hair and the big tits. The two women had been blabbing away while Milo had been thinking about other things.

The blonde nurse had been holding the floor, and the moment Milo pushed the suggestion, she shut her mouth in mid-sentence.

For a second nobody spoke, and then the second nurse, the just slightly overweight one, said, "What is it, Sandy? Is something wr—"

"I've slept with your boyfriend, you know."

Milo smiled deep inside his mind.

"Excuse me? What did you say?"

"You heard me. I've slept with your boyfriend, lots of times. He says you're a nice person and all that, but sex with you is like trying to fuck a dead cow. He says sex with you—"

"Bitch! What the fuck is wrong with you?" The rustle of clothing and an angry grunt indicated to Milo that the girls had begun pushing and shoving each other.

"I'm just telling you the way it is. He says being in the sack with you is like trying to get it up in a freezer, that you're about as cold as—"

A crunching sound told Milo that Overweight Chick had just struck Blondie in the face. And not an openhanded, girlie slap, but a closed-fist, MMA punch to the nose. She was whimpering like a pathetic little girl, but apparently had decided it was time to take action.

The first girl cried out and fell, hitting the floor with a wet smack. Milo pictured her hands clutching her face in a vain attempt to stop the blood now gushing out of her undoubtedly broken nose.

A rush of rubber-soled footsteps told Milo the aggrieved nurse had stepped over her tormentor and hurried out the door. The blonde nurse lay on the floor, moaning and muttering with the thick, distinctive nasal tone of the deviated septum sufferer who was currently bleeding heavily through the nose.

Milo cursed to himself. As much as he enjoyed violence in general and had enjoyed this little tête-à-tête in particular, his intention had been to gain a little quiet time, so he could think and plan. Now he would be forced to listen to this whiny bitch weep and complain.

But not for long. A chorus of raised voices and clatter of activity in the hallway outside his door told Milo someone would be here soon to rescue the suffering nurse. She would be taken from his room and escorted to the ER for medical attention, and her attacker would be...well, he didn't know what the fate of the blonde nurse might be.

Didn't care, either. He had wanted the two tedious little windbags out of his room and he had accomplished that goal, and had had a little fun besides. What could be better?

Now, though, break time was over.

Now it was time to get to work.

5

Milo knew he had to prioritize. There was so much he wanted to do.

The suggestion he pushed into Warden Pender's head had been so easy to accomplish and so goddamned successful in its execution that he was beginning to think he had just scratched the surface of his new-found ability. As much of a burden as living with Flickers had been in his previous incarnation, his current situation was equally ideal.

Immediately following his unsuccessful attempt to rid the world of his odious whore of a twin sister last summer, Milo had wallowed in the depths of despair. Comatose and unable to move, yet fully aware of his surroundings and in considerable pain, he had suspected that his ultimate destiny was finally being realized: he was living in hell on earth.

And he couldn't even end his suffering through suicide.

But then, in a moment of inspiration he would forever cherish as fondly as other people recall their wedding day or the birth of their children, Milo had, quite by accident and without even thinking, *pushed* a suggestion into the head of a young nurse who was busy changing the sheets on his hospital bed. The nurse had immediately dropped to the floor, thrashing and gasping in the throes of a massive orgasm.

And he had been set free.

Now, Milo wouldn't change his situation for all the tea in China, as the expression went. When you could influence people to do your bidding without even lifting a finger, who cared if you were immobile?

Who cared if you were comatose and unresponsive? Who cared about *any* physical limitation?

Not Milo, that was for sure. He was kept clean and nourished, better cared for in this century-and-a-half-old prison/hospital than he had ever cared for himself when he was mobile. And his current situation eliminated distractions, giving him plenty of time to think.

To plan.

To prioritize.

First things first.

He needed to deal with The Evil Bitch Caitlyn Connelly. He hated to admit this, even to himself, but she frightened him. The petite little prim and proper lawyer from the Gulf Coast of Florida, who had probably never smoked a joint or cheated on a test or driven over the fucking speed limit in her whole privileged life, frightened him.

She scared the shit out of him, actually. And the reason was obvious. She possessed his abilities. Or rather, the abilities he had previously manifested before his life-altering shooting. That fact alone made her extremely dangerous. And until he could ensure his twin was out of the way for good, he would never feel safe.

With her dead and buried, his little parlor tricks like forcing people to saw off their own heads—and so much more he had planned—would never be traced back to him. *Could* never be traced back to him. But as long as Caitlyn Connelly walked among the living, Milo's secret was in danger of being revealed. And that was unacceptable.

Her boyfriend would have to be dealt with, too. Milo thought he had killed the wannabe hero once already, back in Revere, but apparently the guy possessed the constitution of a horse. Milo had been forced to listen—over and over, ad nauseum, in those first awful days after being shot, while lying helpless and mostly ignored in his hospital bed—to the incredulous hospital staff's stories of how the dude had miraculously survived his beating and would likely pull through after surgery.

And, of course, he had gone on to do exactly that, adding to Milo's despair and humiliation. But as it turned out, Milo had only lost a battle. The remainder of the war had yet to be fought.

He spent the next several hours considering the Caitlyn Connelly situation from all angles, doing his best to avoid the obvious truth. When he had finished fooling himself, Milo reluctantly concluded that he would have to do what deep down inside he had known all along was the case.

He would have to force a suggestion into Caitlyn Connelly's mind. See if she could resist it any better than Warden Mack Pender had. Finish her.

Move on from there.

REAL ESTATE LAW WAS all about contracts: reading them, writing them, understanding them and applying them. Sometimes Caitlyn felt that after a week of swimming in the *whys* and *wherefores* of real estate contracts for eight to twelve hours a day, by Friday if she were to fall asleep—itself an unlikely proposition, given her insomnia—she would dream about purchase and sales agreements, about escrows and insurance underwriters and all of the other minutiae of her chosen profession.

And she loved it.

She had always craved order and neatness, and polishing a legal document until it was just so, spelling out every last detail so there were no surprises for the buyer or the seller or any intermediaries, was something that never got old for Cait.

Right now, she was working on a lease agreement. A regional drycleaning chain was attempting to establish a foothold in the Tampa Bay area, negotiating the potential lease of a prime downtown location.

The property owner, though, was playing hardball, attempting to extort higher fees than reasonable for market conditions, and Caitlyn had been crafting a response letter on behalf of the dry-cleaning business all morning.

She leaned back in her chair and yawned—another night of inadequate sleep had left her struggling to concentrate—before focusing again on the draft proposal. She was immersed in considering a strategy of agreeing to a slightly higher fee structure in exchange for the property owner guaranteeing availability of other area locations when she gasped. Raised her hands to her head.

Something was wrong.

She could feel...something...happening inside her skull. It wasn't a headache. Not exactly. It wasn't even pain, at least not in the generally accepted sense of the term. It was more like a sense of building pressure, of an invisible air pocket forcing its way into her cranium.

Maybe she was having a stroke. Was that possible? Did reasonably healthy thirty-year-old women suffer strokes? And if so, was this what it would feel like?

Cait didn't think so. She felt normal, aside from that sensation of pressure, which had now leveled off and was definitely noticeable but still not particularly painful. She lifted her arms above her head and shuffled her feet, just to see if she could, and was relieved to discover that she seemed to have retained full control over her extremities.

She reached for the intercom on her desk and buzzed the firm's receptionist, Pearl Hinton. After a moment, a disembodied voice replied, "Yes, Ms. Connelly?"

"Pearl, if you're not too busy, could you come in here for a moment?"

"Of course," came the reply, and seconds later, a soft knock on Cait's office door was followed by the appearance of a tall, thin woman, somewhere between the ages of sixty and eighty, who had been employed at the firm longer than anyone could recall.

"Pearl, I..."

"Yes, ma'am?"

"I'm not sure how to say this, but do I sound...I don't know...normal to you?"

"Normal?"

"Yes. You know, is my diction clear?"

"Your diction."

"Yes." Cait was beginning to regret calling Pearl, but the sensation she experienced had been so disorienting, her immediate reaction had been to try to get some reassurance. Now she just felt silly. "I'm talking all right?"

"Yes, Ms. Connelly, you're talking just fine. Uh...are you *feeling* all right?"

Cait smiled, embarrassed. She could imagine how she must look to this no-nonsense older woman. "Yes, I'm...I'm fine. Would you mind getting me a cup of coffee, please?"

"Coffee. Of course." The woman turned on her heel and marched out of the office, clearly prepared to beat the coffee into submission if necessary.

Cait tried to return her attention to the lease agreement, but her brain would not cooperate. She felt logy, slow. While the feeling of pressure inside her cranium no longer continued to build, it had not dissipated, either.

She struggled with the same sentence three times, growing frustrated, and then Pearl was back at her door. In the receptionist's hands was a large blue ceramic mug emblazoned with the firm's logo, steam rising lazily from the top.

Rattled now, Cait tried to smile. To act normal. She had already made a fool of herself once; she had no intention of doing so again.

Ms. Hinton started across the office, reaching out with the coffee, and then she seemed to stumble. The coffee mug flew from her grasp, floating almost in slow motion through the air, its trajectory putting it on a collision course with Cait's computer. Or possibly Cait herself.

She stuck her hand out, knocking the mug away but of course doing little to impede the progress of the scalding-hot coffee, which had begun splashing out of its container the moment it flew out from Pearl's grasp.

Cait registered a stinging sensation in her hand and forearm as the coffee drenched the sleeve of her blouse before splashing down on her keyboard and computer monitor. She gasped from shock and a millisecond later pain as a single thought flashed through her mind. *She did that on purpose.*

Then two things happened at the same time: the pain from the burns ratcheted up in intensity, and the bizarre sense of pressure in Cait Connelly's head vanished.

6

W*ell.*
That was interesting.

Milo took a moment to relax and allow his thoughts to coalesce. There was much to consider. His experiment had been wildly successful, although it had unfolded much differently than he expected it to.

For whatever reason, he could not push suggestions into The Evil Bitch's brain. Whatever strange psychic connection they shared as twin brother and sister apparently precluded any possibility of him forcing her to cut her head off with a letter opener, or to do anything at all according to his bidding.

Unfortunate.

However, the plus side of the equation was filled with interesting tidbits. Things that, on balance, more than made up for his disappointment in finding out he could not manipulate his nemesis into performing a gruesome suicidal attack on herself while he lay motionless in his hospital bed fifteen hundred miles away.

When he had pushed his suggestion into the nurse's brain, and then again when he had achieved his greatest accomplishment thus far, pushing the suggestion of suicide into Warden Pender's head, he had focused on the specific people in his mind. He envisioned them even though he had never actually seen either one. The very fact that he had interacted with them, however passively on his part, seemed to have been enough to forge the kind of psychic connection required for the implantation process.

He already knew he could not push suggestions into the minds of people he'd never interacted with. People like the United States president, Hollywood actors and actresses. He had tried numerous times with them and others, always to no avail.

But that wasn't a problem with Caitlyn Connelly. It had been even easier to focus on her than it had been on the nurses or Mack Pender. Connelly's face—her entire odious being, really—was burned indelibly into his consciousness. He knew he would see her in his nightmares until the day he died. His contempt for her was utter and unrelenting.

But although picturing her had been a breeze, the process of implanting a suggestion remained impossible. Instead, when he had *pushed* with his mind, he was rewarded with something entirely unexpected: he could see through her eyes.

Instantly, his mind was filled with the sights and sounds of her vantage point. She was sitting at a desk upon which stacks of forms and official-looking documents had been placed, and she was working on something on her computer. It was a letter of some sort, comprised of lawyerly mumbo-jumbo the likes of which held absolutely no interest to Milo Cain.

But the vantage point, that was another story. He could see through her eyes!

Connelly had known immediately that something was wrong; Milo could sense it. But she had no idea what that something might be, and why would she? Nothing in her life, not even her experience with Flickers and her deadly run-in with Milo back in Revere last summer, could have prepared her for her cranium being invaded by a comatose cripple, incarcerated and largely forgotten, all the way up the Atlantic coast.

And while that was fascinating—who wouldn't want to see the world through someone else's eyes for a while?—what had happened next was truly magical. The flustered Connelly, embarrassed and confused about what was wrong, had requested a cup of coffee she didn't really want as a way to get the unwanted attention of the ancient hag of a secretary off her.

When the wrinkled bitch returned with the coffee, Milo had, almost randomly and on the spur of the moment, pushed a suggestion *through* Connelly and into the head of the old lady. And to his immense surprise, it worked. Milo's suggestion was for the lady to trip and spill the full-to-the-brim coffee cup all over the evil Connelly bitch, *and she had done exactly that!*

Whether the secretary had slipped or tripped or dumped the coffee without even knowing why she would do such a thing, the scalding-hot liquid flew through the air, as pretty as you please, and burned The Evil Bitch.

Exactly as he had intended.

But something else had happened, too, something that was equally unexpected. He had been overcome by exhaustion. Milo exited Connelly's head immediately, partly because he felt he had gained all the knowledge he was likely to from his little experiment, but mostly because he was suddenly so tired he knew he needed to rest and recover.

Apparently, invading his twin sister's skull required a much greater expenditure of psychic energy than did simply implanting a suggestion in an unwitting recipient's brain. After only a few minutes spent observing the world through Caitlyn Connelly's eyes, and then especially after forcing a suggestion through her head and into the secretary's brain, Milo felt drained, utterly enervated.

He knew instinctively that to remain inside The Evil Bitch's skull for much longer would have resulted in...what? Exhaustion? Unconsciousness? Death?

Milo wasn't sure *what* would have happened had he overstayed his welcome, but he knew he didn't want to find out. Right now he needed to recover, to regain his strength, to celebrate this odd victory and consider its ramifications.

It was a minor achievement, to be sure. Spilling coffee on your hated enemy's arm would not exactly qualify as winning the war, even if you did manage to inflict second-degree burns. But the experiment was significant not for what it accomplished but rather for the possibilities it opened up.

There were so many possibilities. And they all revolved around the destruction of Caitlyn Connelly.

7

Caitlyn's arm throbbed, despite being slathered in antibacterial burn cream and covered with gauze wrap. Pearl hurried to her in a panic after spilling the coffee, eyes wide, apologizing profusely for her clumsiness. She took one look at the damage and picked up Cait's phone, dialing 911.

Caitlyn immediately canceled the call for the ambulance. There was no way she was going to the hospital. She was too busy for that.

"It's fine," she told Pearl. "We have first-aid supplies here. I'll dress the burn and keep it clean and it'll be good as new in a few days."

Pearl looked dubious. She gazed at the burn with obvious skepticism, but to Cait's relief did not argue the point. After helping Cait dress the wound, maintaining a near-continuous stream of apologies, Pearl finally left the office and returned to her desk, which was really what Cait had wanted all along.

She needed some time to think.

Something strange was happening, that much was obvious, but what in the heck it might be she had no idea.

She cleaned her computer's keyboard the best she could, suspecting that once the spilled coffee finished dripping through the case and into the electronics, it would be a goner. After saving and backing up all her work, she made another attempt at completing the disputed lease agreement, but after a few minutes, Cait was forced to give up and admit defeat.

Her concentration was shot. And more importantly, her arm was killing her. It was Friday afternoon and she'd already put in nearly sixty hours this week, so given all that had happened, Cait felt she was more than justified in cutting out early and going home. She would relax for a while, maybe pamper herself with a bubble bath, and would still have time to surprise Kevin with something special for dinner.

She deserved a little time to herself.

THE LASAGNA WAS COOLING in a pan on top of the stove when Kevin walked into their apartment.

He mock-checked his watch. "Well, this is a pleasant surprise," he said enthusiastically. "My sweetheart is home and it's not even nine o'clock yet!"

"Home," she said, "*and* I've been cooking like Betty Crocker. If I was any more domesticated, I'd never go back to work."

"Smells delicious," Kevin said. "But where's my martini?"

"What are you talking about?"

"Isn't that what the truly domesticated little woman is supposed to do? Meet her man at the door, hand him a drink and then hang up his suit coat?"

Cait grinned. "Good luck with that. And besides, you don't wear a suit."

"Hmph. Seems like you need more practice at this 'little woman' stuff," he said, laughing, as he dodged a punch. "But seriously, what's the occasion? You're never home this early."

Cait decided to downplay the strange events of the afternoon. The odd sensation of pressure inside her skull hadn't returned, and as the hours went by it became easier to pass the bizarre occurrence off as nothing more than some weird trick of her mind. She was tired all the time thanks to her insomnia; maybe this afternoon was just her body reacting to her constant state of exhaustion.

But there was no hiding the burn. She rolled up her sleeve and Kevin blinked in confusion and then looked at her questioningly. "What the hell happened to you?"

"Coffee accident. And you think being a cop is a dangerous job. Try working in a law office."

"With all those sharks? No thanks. I'll take my chances on the street. But if you spilled coffee on yourself, how did you manage to burn your arm almost all the way to the elbow?"

Cait explained about Pearl tripping and the coffee flying through the air, leaving out the conviction she had felt at the time that the older woman had done it intentionally. That notion was plainly ridiculous. Cait had worked with Pearl Hinton for almost three years and while the woman could be frosty, she had never treated Cait with anything but the utmost professional courtesy.

Kevin listened without speaking, and when Cait finished the story, his face remained a mask of cop skepticism. She knew the expression well.

"What is it?" she asked.

"The woman slipped walking across a carpeted floor and the coffee ended up burning *you*? How far away was she when this happened?"

Cait shrugged. "I don't know. Five or six feet, I guess."

Kevin stared at her without speaking and finally she spread her hands apart in frustration. Sometimes living with a cop could be tiring. "What?"

"Doesn't it strike you as, I don't know, a little *unlikely* that someone could slip badly enough to launch a full cup of coffee at a person sitting five or six feet away? We've all spilled coffee before, but when it happens, who usually takes the brunt of the spill?"

"Well...the person carrying the coffee."

"Exactly. Did Pearl fall? How badly did *she* get burned?"

Cait shook her head. "None of the coffee landed on her."

"You see where I'm coming from?"

"I do," Cait said, recalling again her fleeting thought that the secretary had engineered the spill on purpose. "But it's over now. Let's forget about it and enjoy dinner."

Kevin wasn't quite ready to let the subject drop. "She needs to be more careful. Thank God it wasn't your other arm that got scalded. I'm no doctor, but I'm guessing a burn like that would be bad news for those still-healing skin grafts."

Cait nodded. She had considered that issue, too. "All's well that ends well," she said brightly. "Now, let's eat before the lasagna gets cold."

At that moment, the pressure in her head returned with a vengeance.

THE TIMING OF HIS RETURN into The Evil Bitch's head couldn't have been better if he had spent months planning it. Milo took his good fortune as a sign that fate was on his side. Cait Connelly was home, and even better, her wannabe-hero cop boyfriend was there as well.

This was perfect. Because there was more than one way to skin a cat. Milo could not push a suggestion into his whore sister's brain and cause her to kill herself like he had done with Warden Pender, but that didn't matter now. He would adapt and overcome.

He was clever that way.

8

Caitlyn raised her hands to her head exactly as she had done sitting at her desk earlier in the day. The pressure was immense and she stumbled forward a step or two, her body sagging. A small jolt of pain ripped through her skull.

She moaned and reached for Kevin, grabbing at his uniform shirt with both hands. Thank God he was home. He was big and strong and could easily support the weight of her small form. He would help her.

She waited for him to take hold of her staggering body, waited for him to gasp in surprise or to ask what was wrong or to do *anything,* but he stood wooden, unmoving. Cait sagged to her knees, her fingers losing their tenuous grip on Kevin's shirt. She looked up at his face and saw that he was gazing down at her blankly.

"Kevin," she said, not knowing how to continue. The pressure in her cranium seemed to have stabilized and now that the initial shock of her head being invaded—that was what it felt like, an invasion—was wearing off, Cait rallied slightly. The initial sensation of pain had disappeared.

She placed her hands on the floor and pushed off, struggling to regain her footing. At that moment she felt herself being lifted roughly. Kevin had grabbed her under her armpits and was hauling her upright.

"Take it easy," she said, shaking her head as he lifted her and then dropped her onto her feet. She felt dizzy and disoriented.

He said nothing in response. Instead, he placed both hands on her upper chest, just below her shoulder blades, and *shoved* her hard. She flew backward, smashing into the wall and rattling a framed photograph of her and Kevin on vacation in Tahiti that had been taken two winters ago. The picture banged against the wall once and dislodged from its mounting. It fell and the glass inside the frame shattered, scattering shards across the floor like a sprinkling of snow.

Cait crumpled to the floor, stunned, too surprised even to scream. She had known Kevin Dalton for six years and in all that time he had never once touched her in anger. But now he leaned down and grabbed a fistful of her blouse, yanking her off the floor in an explosive burst.

Silk ripped and buttons scattered, bouncing randomly among the glass on the floor. *This is a brand-new blouse,* Cait thought absurdly, *and now it's ruined.*

And then Kevin slugged her, striking her in the side of the head with the base of an open hand but knocking her once more against the wall, scrambling her circuits. Her vision flickered like lights in a thunderstorm. From somewhere far away, she heard another crash and registered it as the bathroom mirror falling and smashing on the sink.

She slid to the floor and lay stunned, taking vague notice of blood trickling onto the hardwood.

She had sliced herself falling onto broken glass.

That was the least of her problems.

After a stretch of silence that might have been five seconds or ten minutes—Cait was too stunned and confused to know—she once again felt herself being lifted into the air. She blinked rapidly in a desperate attempt to clear her spinning head as Kevin half carried, half dragged her down the hallway and into the living room.

He dumped her onto their couch. Then he drew his service weapon from its holster and, impossibly, aimed it at her head.

She stared in shock and horror at the barrel of his gun, its open end pointing into her face. From this perspective it looked as big as a cannon.

Cait had never felt unsafe with a firearm in their apartment; in fact, the reality was just the opposite. Kevin Dalton was a cop. He was responsible and professional. He kept his weapon locked in a gun safe while at home and Cait had always felt *more* secure with the knowledge that the weapon was here and available to him, not less.

But now she stared into the gaping maw of the barrel, too surprised to be afraid.

Yet.

What the hell was happening? One minute she was smiling and joking with her longtime boyfriend, just another Friday night at home, and the next he went crazy, attacking her, striking her multiple times, and now threatening her with deadly violence.

He spoke, and through her ringing ears the sound was utterly unlike his normal voice. The total lack of inflection was nothing she had ever heard out of another human being. Certainly not out of Kevin, whose normal tone was warm and silky. The vocal transformation was just as unexpected as the sudden, vicious attack.

"Make one move off that couch and you die," he said. "I'll put a bullet right between your pretty blue eyes. Do you understand me?"

Cait was too shocked to answer. This couldn't be happening. It just could not.

Then he said, "Well?"

She nodded once. "I understand," she said, although she didn't. She didn't come close to understanding.

"Good," Kevin—or whatever it was—answered. He stood motionless for another minute. Then two.

Cait felt blood trickling down the side of her face.

She felt her eyes begin filling with tears.

And then her attacker turned and walked into the kitchen. A second later, Cait heard drawers being opened, utensils being dumped onto the floor.

She tried to control her rapidly rising panic. She had to make absolutely the right choices from this point on or she would likely die. She might die anyway.

That monster digging through the silverware in their kitchen was not Kevin. The man she lived with, made love to, and trusted more intimately than anyone else in the world would not treat her like this.

Kevin would not assault her and threaten her and point a loaded gun at her.

So she would have to treat him not like Kevin Dalton, the man she loved, but like a stranger with an unknown agenda and uncertain motives. She would have to treat him like...she flashed on Milo Cain, leaning over her prone body in her mother's house in Revere, calmly peeling the skin away from her forearm. The similarities between the two situations were startling. But Milo Cain lay in a prison hospital fifteen hundred miles away, comatose and helpless, nothing more than a bad memory, left behind to rot in her past where he belonged.

She snapped back to the present and pictured their apartment's front door, no more than twenty feet away, a slab of reinforced metal beckoning with the promise of freedom.

Maybe she could make it. She would have to climb off the couch, race down the hallway and past the kitchen, and then pull the door open before he could catch her from behind or shoot her in the back as she passed.

Had Kevin locked the door when he came home? She didn't know, but guessed he probably had. He was a cop, after all, obsessed as all cops seemed to be with safety and security.

Of course he had locked the door. For him *not* to have locked it would represent a shift in character every bit as significant for him as what was going on right now. So she would have to unlock the door, too, before escaping. That would take precious time.

And just getting into the hallway would not be enough. Unless one of her neighbors happened to be entering or exiting their apartment and she could convince them to let her in and then lock the door be-hind them, the hallway would provide no margin of safety. She would be a sitting duck; the Kevin-thing could overtake her or shoot her with-out even breaking a sweat.

Still, it might be her only chance.

Anything would be better than lying here waiting for...whatever was going to happen next.

She would have to risk it.

She started to swing her legs onto the floor. The adrenaline filled her system like it was being pumped into her through a fire hose. Her head swam, she felt dizzy and weak from the beating she had taken.

Fight or flight. She had to try.

And then the opportunity was gone, because Kevin Dalton—or whatever Kevin had suddenly become—was back. She had missed out on what might be her only chance to escape an unknown fate. What probably *would* be her only chance.

He stood in the doorway studying her, hands clasped behind his back, his eyes somehow simultaneously blank and calculating.

"What's this all about?" Cait said, speaking softly, knowing her on-ly chance was to try to gain the upper hand. If that was even possible. Get him talking and keep him talking.

"This is about unfinished business," the Kevin-thing said. "This is about putting people in their place and teaching them to keep their noses out of things that don't concern them." His voice rumbled from deep inside his chest, sounding completely unlike the man she knew. He sounded like some bizarre cyborg straight out of a low-budget sci-ence-fiction movie, the strange lack of inflection both terrifying and in-explicable. The sound no more resembled Kevin's voice than his actions represented his normal personality.

Cait's mind raced and she tried to focus on nothing but the need to keep this monster talking. She noticed he had holstered his gun and took that as a positive sign.

"Where did I put my nose that didn't concern me?" She tried to keep her voice steady and more or less succeeded.

The Kevin-thing smiled. The effect was ghastly. It was like a Halloween mask had been slipped over Kevin's face and was now rearranging itself into the rough approximation of a human smile. There was absolutely no warmth attached to the gesture. "That's irrelevant to the current situation. You need to be taught a lesson and so you will be."

Cait breathed deeply. "How can I learn a lesson if I don't know what I did wrong?"

The Kevin-thing removed one hand from behind its back and flicked it like a man shooing away a fly. "I told you. It's irrelevant. Try to pay attention. You won't be leaving this apartment alive, so whether you are aware of your transgressions or not doesn't matter in the least. Now, shall we get started?"

The Kevin-thing moved forward. He removed his other hand from behind his back.

He was holding a carving knife.

It glittered in the artificial light of the living room as he walked.

9

Milo's excitement was almost more than he could bear. He had never felt more alive than he did at this moment. Not while peeling the skin off his previous victims, not while playing mind games with Caitlyn Connelly last summer back in Revere.

Never. If he had been capable of achieving an erection, he knew he would be sporting blue steel right now. He was finally going to accomplish what he had failed at once already, and what he had dreamt about in lonely solitude every single day since being shot in the face.

At last, Caitlyn Connelly would be made to pay for her refusal to submit, for injuring him so severely he would forever remain a broken and forgotten throwaway in this one-hundred-fifty-year-old shithole of a prison. For being the object of his overwhelming, unrelenting, fiery hatred.

And the wait had been worth every minute. Because now, not only could he control every move her wannabe-hero boyfriend made, thus achieving a certain payback with him as well, he had the added bonus of *being able to see everything as it happened!*

He sat inside Cait's head, gazing out through her eyeballs, seeing everything she saw in real time, as she saw it. He had watched, spell-bound, as the apartment careened sideways when Connelly's boyfriend smashed her into the wall, not once, but twice, all on Milo's suggestion, of course. He had watched in amusement as Kevin Dalton returned from the kitchen, hands behind his back, waiting for the proper moment to spring the little surprise of the knife on her.

And now he watched through her terrified eyes as Dalton slowly moved next to her and knelt, squatting on his haunches, displaying the carving knife inches from her face. Her reaction was everything he could have hoped for and more. It was like the announcer in that stupid credit card commercial said: *Priceless.*

Her eyesight jiggled and stuttered as her body shook, convulsing in terror at the unexpected appearance of the knife. She glanced around the room in a panic, obviously looking for something, anything, with which to defend herself.

But there was nothing.

She was at his mercy.

And this time there would be no interruption. He could proceed at a leisurely pace, take his time and do things right, draw the process out. Keep her alive as long as possible to prolong his enjoyment. No one would interrupt. The only other person who could possibly interfere, Kevin Dalton, was already here and would continue to do Milo's bidding, presumably for as long as he desired.

Milo's only regret was that he would not get to experience the enjoyment of *watching* the actual damage as Connelly suffered, except for those few occasions when she happened to glance down at the knife work. He felt confident those moments would be rare. She would not want to see.

But that was a minor quibble, one he could easily make up for using his imagination and those beautiful images he had stored in his memory from past exploits with the prostitutes and those all-too-few college girls he had permitted himself to enjoy.

And, of course, her.

He sighed with satisfaction—in his mind—and watched through The Evil Bitch's eyes as Dalton finished displaying the knife to his victim.

"Now," he said, the voice rumbling and strange, neither Milo's nor Dalton's, but rather some weird hybrid monster-voice. "How shall we proceed? Shall we begin with your previously damaged arm? It seems to have begun healing quite well, but I have to assume there will be plenty of extra pain involved once those grafts start peeling off.

"Or would it be better to start on the other side? Those coffee burns courtesy of your impossibly clumsy secretary look so inviting, so red and raw and painful, that it's almost like a neon sign advertising, 'Slice Here, Slice Here!' It's quite the dilemma, don't you agree?"

"Why are you doing this?" Connelly whispered. Her voice shook and it turned him on.

"Please," he said dismissively. "We've been over this already. The things that got us to this point are water under the bridge. Do try and keep up. You're a lawyer, for crissakes, so I know you have at least some small intellectual capacity."

"It...it's you," she said, her whisper now even softer, eyes darting everywhere, her mind clearly teetering on the precipice of madness. "It's you, isn't it?"

"Whatever do you mean?"

"Never mind why you're doing this. *How* are you doing it?"

Milo pushed a suggestion into Dalton to smile. He could tell by Connelly's steadfast refusal to look straight at it that the result must be horrifying. He did his best to make the answer sound taunting, amused, but it mostly just came out in that awful robotic tone: "How am I doing it? The answer should be obvious, even to someone as...limited...as you. I'm holding a knife to your throat and in a moment I'm going to use the knife to carve you."

"That's not what I mean," Connelly whispered. "You're...you're...him..." She couldn't bring herself to say his name, but there was no question to whom she was referring.

Milo smiled inside and had Kevin continue as if she had not spoken. "The fact of the matter is I'm sick and tired of your Miss Goody-Two-Shoes act. That wholesome, All-American Girl shit is really wearing thin. You need to learn how to get down and dirty, to swim around in the muck and the mud with the rest of us."

Milo could sense Connelly tensing up, could feel a simmering anger joining the fear festering inside her. "You're *not Kevin*," she hissed. "Kevin would never—"

She gasped as Milo implanted a suggestion in Dalton's brain to lower the tip of the knife to the delicate skin of her throat, just below her ear and above her jawbone. He had had enough of her incessant whining. It was time to get started.

She stopped speaking and whimpered softly and Milo thought it was just about the sweetest sound he had ever heard. In the back of his mind, he wondered what would happen if he were still inside Caitlyn Connelly's head when she finally stopped breathing. Would he die too?

But that was a worry for much later. He was going to make damned sure she stayed alive—and conscious—for a good long while. Days, if possible. He would be sure to jump out of her head before the end, just in case, but for now he had much more enjoyable things to think about.

He knew he would have to restrain her, to tie her down securely in order for him to do his best work. And, most importantly, he needed to gag her. Soon. This was no abandoned tenement building in one of the most decrepit areas of downtown Boston. This was a ritzy, fancy-Dan high-rise apartment building on the Gulf Coast of Florida. There were probably several thousand people within a few hundred feet of them right this very moment.

But first things first. He couldn't help himself. He just had to give this uptight, righteous bitch a little taste of what she had to look forward to over the next couple of days. Nothing much, just a taste.

Dalton was still holding the knife at the bitch's throat, and now Milo pushed the suggestion to move it away from her neck and down to her arm. He didn't specify which arm—didn't particularly care which one got cut first; he would end up slicing both eventually, anyway—and Dalton chose the burned one.

He grabbed the arm with one hand to hold it steady. With the other, he lowered the point of the knife down to the creamy white skin of the inner forearm, just above the raw, red scalded area, still wrapped in bandages.

Milo had him push down with gentle pressure.

The bitch jumped and gasped and stared directly at the affected area.

"Scream, and I'll slit your throat from ear to ear," he had Dalton say in that oddly robotic voice. "You'll be dead before anyone even knows something is wrong. Do you understand?"

Connelly said nothing. She continued to stare as if mesmerized at the knife blade resting lightly on the skin of her forearm. Her vision was jumpy. Her terror was plain. Milo was ecstatic.

"Do you understand?"

"I...I...yes, I understand," she said, her voice breaking. She was on the verge of panic.

Milo pushed a suggestion to his inadvertent accomplice and watched as the tip of the blade dimpled the skin slightly, and then broke through.

The bitch exhaled violently like she had been holding her breath. "Ahhh," she moaned quietly.

"No screams," Milo had Kevin say to the terrified young woman, and then pushed a suggestion to remove the knife. Dalton lifted the blade and a perfect crimson pearl of blood welled up in the tiny puncture, hesitated a moment at the opening as if unsure how to proceed, and then overflowed the hole and followed gravity's path, trickling sluggishly down the arm.

And then Connelly's eyes shifted away from the impromptu artwork and up to the face of the man subjecting her to this torture. Milo felt a flash of anger and an almost physical sense of loss at the change in perspective. There was nothing more beautiful in this world as far as Milo Cain was concerned than observing the effects of a razor-sharp blade slicing into living human flesh.

"Please," she said.

Milo ignored the whimpers of the pathetic creature. Where was her desire for restraint when she had been pointing the barrel of a handgun in his face? Where was her interest in nonviolence when she pulled the trigger, pulverizing his skull and rendering him a nonresponsive lump of skin and bone? Where was it then? Where?

Milo felt the familiar sense of rage building rapidly, the desire to commit mindless violence on her, to eradicate the stain of her presence from the face of the earth. It was always the same where Caitlyn Connelly was concerned. Every time he saw or even just thought about his twin sister, the devil incarnate, he was overcome with the compulsion to slash, to cut, to kill.

He had thought he could control it now, thought that by orchestrating events from many hundreds of miles away, while his physical presence lay comatose and unmoving, he would be better able to think rationally.

He had been wrong.

The simmering fury had been tamped down for a few minutes, but now it was back, flashing like a campfire doused with gasoline. Milo discovered he could no longer even remember *why* he had wanted to contain it. He was never more at home than when in the grip of mindless rage, and now he surrendered to it.

Somewhere deep in the recesses of his mind, he tried to reason with himself, tried to tell himself that he wanted to draw this out, to make it last, to force the Connelly bitch to suffer as he had suffered for so long, but at the same time he knew it was not going to happen. Self-control had never been Milo Cain's strong point and that didn't seem likely to change now.

He pushed a suggestion to Connelly's wannabe-hero boyfriend, and the instrument of Milo's revenge instantly obeyed, as Milo had known he would. He rotated his wrist so the blade of the carving knife was hovering over Connelly's forearm, less than an inch above the skin.

Dalton lowered the knife and without warning pressed it into the skin slightly. He began peeling like a baker removing the skin from an apple.

Milo cursed inside his head. Dalton was following instructions to the best of his ability, but his technique was clumsy, he had no idea what he was doing. To Milo, a virtuoso with a carving knife, his expertise born of hundreds of hours of practice and experimentation on dozens of victims, the result was sloppy, ineffective. Pointless.

The knife slipped out of Connelly's arm as the boyfriend failed to maintain the required pressure on the blade.

Milo's fury threatened to overwhelm him. He angrily pushed a suggestion to the good-for-nothing Tampa cop to try again, but before the man could comply, two things happened in rapid succession:

Caitlyn Connelly screamed.

And an angry pounding of authoritative fists sounded at the apartment's front door.

10

At first, Cait didn't hear the banging on the door. She had been trying her hardest to remain under control, not so much as a result of the Kevin-thing's threat to cut her throat if she didn't, but rather because she was convinced that doing so represented her only chance for survival.

But then that knife blade bit cleanly into her arm, the obvious intention being to remove the skin exactly as had been done to her in Revere last summer, and everything came flooding back: the sheer unreasoning terror, the white-hot flamethrower blast of pain radiating from the rough incision, all of it made worse by the knowledge that the outrage was being committed by the very man who, up until a few minutes ago, she had trusted more than anyone in the world. Had trusted with her life.

All conscious thought vanished.

And she screamed.

Not a tentative, *please don't hurt me* scream, but a full-throated, six-year-old-caught-in-the-grip-of-a-horrible-nightmare scream, long and loud and lusty. She simply could not help herself.

Suddenly the knife slipped out of her arm, leaving in its wake an obscene gouge from which the blood poured, instantly soaking both Cait's clothing and the material of the couch, a fact that barely registered to her panicked mind.

She panted and took a breath and went to scream again, and that was when she heard the fists pounding on the door. Then the banging stopped and was followed immediately by an angry voice, loud and insistent. "Tampa police! Open up right now or we're kicking this door in!"

Instantly the pressure inside Cait's skull vanished. It was like the air being let out of a balloon. Next to her, Kevin abruptly lost his balance and fell. He pushed himself up onto his knees, eyes blank, body stiff and cumbersome.

The angry voice outside the door said, "Open up!"

Seconds passed in total silence. Kevin shook his head, blinking rapidly. He looked like a little boy who had been awakened suddenly from a nap. He picked the bloody knife up off the floor and gazed at it stupidly, then glanced from it to Cait's arm and back again as if in utter incomprehension.

Then chaos.

A sharp *Crack!* from down the hallway was followed by the sound of the front door smashing into the wall as the police made good on their threat to break it down. The pounding of heavy footsteps filled the apartment as Kevin rose to his feet. He looked pale and shaky. He turned sluggishly toward the commotion and as he did the home was filled with shouted voices reverberating off the walls:

"Police! Stop right there!"

"Get down on the floor right now!"

"Nobody move!"

Cait slid off the couch, landing on her knees in the exact spot Kevin had occupied until seconds ago. She cradled her bleeding arm against her chest and peered toward the source of the commotion.

And her breath caught in her throat.

Kevin was stumbling down the hallway toward the smashed-in front door, where three cops clustered just inside the apartment. Two had dropped into shooter's crouches and one stood just behind them, legs spread for balance. All had their weapons drawn, and all were pointing those weapons down the hallway.

At Kevin.

Who continued toward them, knife in his hand, blood dripping from the blade onto the carpet.

The cops were screaming at him, *"Drop the knife and lie facedown on the floor!"* Their voices were adrenaline-fueled, intense and insistent.

And Kevin kept coming. He bounced off the hallway wall, broken glass crunching under his feet, and continued toward the cops. He seemed disoriented, and Cait knew what was about to happen even if he didn't.

"Don't shoot!" she screamed, her voice shrill and high-pitched and lost in the confusion.

"Last chance," one cop screamed. "Drop the knife right now!"

Kevin slowed but didn't stop. He was gripping the knife in his right hand, held down by his waist, and he stared at it again as if seeing it for the first time. Then he lifted it to get a better look, and that was the worst thing he could have done, and Cait screamed "Noooo," and one of the cops fired, and Kevin spun around as if he had been hit by a car, and then Cait was sobbing and screaming and Kevin lay on the hallway floor, bleeding from the shoulder and unmoving.

11

Milo Cain was rattled. He didn't like to admit it because to do so indicated a disconnect between reality and his carefully constructed self-image. He was clever and smart, always one step—at a minimum—ahead of law enforcement, and several steps ahead of everyone else.

What had happened in Revere last summer was an aberration, nothing more. Milo had successfully selected, kidnapped and tortured many victims over the course of more than a decade prior to being shot in the face in Revere, and he knew the shooting and his subsequent capture and imprisonment—inside his now worthless body as well as here at Bridgewater State Hospital—was nothing more than the worst kind of bad luck.

After discovering his new powers, Milo had felt strong and omnipotent once again, especially following the smashing success of his experiment on Warden Pender.

So when he had pushed the suggestion into wannabe-hero Kevin Dalton's thick skull to attack and then carve up the she-devil Caitlyn Connelly, he had had every expectation things would proceed as planned.

Then it all fell apart, beginning with his inability to control his white-hot fury at his Goody-Two-Shoes twin. Then he had been frustrated and angered by the dolt Dalton's inability to maintain anything close to proper knife control, no sooner sinking the blade into the girl's arm than seeing it pop right out again like a dolphin jumping out of the water at fucking SeaWorld.

But then when the goddamn police came busting through Connelly's front door, hell-bent on saving the day, he completely dropped the ball. As much as it pained Milo to admit it, the facts were the facts, and he had panicked.

There were so many ways he could have handled the situation, all of which would have resulted in a decent outcome:

He could have ignored the pigs and pushed a suggestion to Dalton to plunge the carving knife straight into Connelly's heart. It would have eliminated his dream of playing with the girl, of torturing her and making her suffer as long as he possibly could, that much was true. But at least she would have been dead.

He could have pushed a different suggestion into the wannabe hero's brain, to leap up and attack the cops at the door, charging straight at them with the knife held high while screaming like a banshee. He would certainly have been cut down in a hail of bullets, and while that result would have left Connelly unharmed, it would have accomplished almost as much on the torture front as peeling the skin off her arm would have.

Milo had seen her devotion to the idiot Kevin Dalton up close, and he resented it like he resented everything else about Miss Polly Purebred.

There were so many ways he could have handled the situation, and he had done none of them. He lost his nerve, surprised by the cavalry's arrival, and turned tail and ran, jumping out of Connelly's head like a coward and retreating into his prone body here in the hospital bed at Bridgewater.

He tried to console himself, to make the best of a bad situation and convince himself that it wasn't a total loss. By the time the pigs started pounding on Connelly's front door, his energy had been rapidly waning, anyway. He had been weakening fast, and the fact of the matter was that he could only have managed a couple more minutes inside The Evil Bitch's skull before risking...whatever the result of overstaying his welcome would be.

So really, Milo reasoned, escaping Connelly's head had been inevitable. He would have had to do so even had the cops *not* shown up. In some ways, their arrival may have been a blessing. He had been so wrapped up in extracting his revenge from the self-righteous little bitch, so filled with anger and vengeance, that he hadn't really noticed himself growing steadily weaker.

If he was being honest with himself—which he always tried to be because as far as Milo was concerned, honesty was the key to self-knowledge—he couldn't be one hundred percent certain he would have possessed the awareness to get out in time.

The more Milo thought about it, the more he realized the Tampa Police Department might have done him a huge favor. They may, however unwittingly, have saved him from himself.

After escaping Connelly's skull, Milo popped back into his own broken body, his own misshapen cranium, and dropped almost immediately into a deep, dreamless sleep. He had been as exhausted as he could ever recall being, even more than the times he had spent close to forty-eight hours straight torturing his pretty victims, foregoing sleep because he was simply having so much goddamned fun.

The irony was inescapable. Here was a man comatose, a man the entire world thought to be in some kind of limbo, caught between the living and the dead. As far as the medical community was concerned, Milo Cain could see nothing, hear nothing, experience nothing.

In reality, the opposite was true. While Milo could not see, he could hear and understand perfectly everything that was going on around him even if he was incapable of responding.

After his psychic journey inside Caitlyn Connelly, however, Milo actually *became* the unresponsive lump of flesh everyone already thought him to be. Had he not been paralyzed already, he would have seemed so, anyway.

Milo had no way of knowing exactly how long he spent unconscious and recovering from his psychic journey, but he guessed it was probably close to a day. When he awoke, he felt refreshed and alert, ready for wherever the next steps of his plan for vengeance against Caitlyn Connelly might take him.

To anyone who might have entered his hospital room and looked at him, there was no difference now than there had been before. His body still huddled unmoving under the thin prison blankets, the only evidence of his continued life being the steady rise and fall of his chest.

But Milo could feel the difference, and that was what mattered.

The first thing he did upon awakening was to journey back into Connelly's head. He was careful not to overstay his welcome—yet—but it was important to learn the specifics of what had happened after his panicked departure.

What he learned filled his heart with happiness. He discovered that Kevin Dalton, while still unfortunately alive, had indeed been shot by the police—the first thing the pigs had ever done right as far as Milo was concerned, and probably the *only* time in his life they would ever be on the same side—and was currently being held under police guard in a hospital bed recovering from his wounds.

The Evil Bitch had been patched up—again—and was continuing on like the goddamn bunny in those battery commercials. She just kept going and going and going. Milo felt the bile rising in his chest. It was disgusting.

After tamping down the rage already beginning to build inside him, Milo leaped out of Connelly's head again and back into his own. He could not afford the downtime it would take to recover from another extended stay in Connelly's skull.

Upon his return, Milo again felt tired and weak. It wasn't anything like the exhaustion he had experienced following Kevin Dalton's attack on Connelly, but it *was* significant. Milo congratulated himself on his ability to stick to the plan. He had learned something important: these psychic journeys inside The Evil Bitch's head did not come without a price.

He hoped they took a toll on her just as they did on him.

While he rested and recovered from this latest excursion, Milo considered all that he had experienced so far, especially Caitlyn Connelly's seeming penchant for escaping certain death. Supposedly cats had nine lives, but Milo was beginning to think Connelly might as well.

However, with the luxury of a little time and some calm reflection, Milo decided that whether Connelly had one life or nine lives or nine hundred, it didn't matter. Because Milo Cain wasn't going anywhere. He would regroup and plan, and then try again.

He was nothing if not persistent.

He would get what he wanted in the end: the destruction of The Evil Bitch Caitlyn Connelly.

12

I t was well past midnight by the time Caitlyn got home. A trip to the emergency room to have her arm sutured had been followed by a question-and-answer session with a Tampa police detective:

No, she and Kevin had not been arguing prior to the attack.

No, she did not know what had set Kevin off.

No, he had never struck her before or been abusive to her in any way.

Cait could tell with utter certainty that the detective—a tired-looking middle-aged man named Santos—didn't believe her. He wasn't sure whether she was lying out of fear or to protect her man or for some other unknown reason, but every denial she issued resulted in pursed lips or an impatient clearing of the throat or a very slight shake of the head.

Cait didn't blame the man. She wouldn't have believed her story, either, had she been sitting on the other side of the table. An attack of this severity didn't just come out of nowhere without warning. Happy couples not experiencing problems did not suddenly start carving each other up on their living room couch.

The interview went on for a while, Detective Santos rephrasing things, circling around to the same questions, doing his damnedest to get Cait to admit that yes, Kevin had been assaulting her for years, had been abusing her and humiliating her and beating her.

Despite his best efforts, Cait stuck to her story because it was the truth. What else would she say?

After a while Detective Santos seemed to recognize he wasn't going to make any headway with the damn fool victim. He sat for a moment and sighed, and said, "You know, Ms. Connelly, we can't protect you if you won't accept our help."

"What's going to happen to Kevin?" she asked, ignoring Santos's statement because it was obvious he didn't want to hear her denials.

"That's up to the D.A.," he said. "In my view we have enough evidence to bring a charge of attempted murder, but that hasn't been determined yet. We're still trying to get to the bottom of what happened." Left unsaid was his implication: that the obstinate victim of the attack was making the quest for justice much more difficult than it needed to be.

Cait didn't care. He could have said it out loud and she still wouldn't have cared. This guy was a colleague of Kevin's—maybe they even knew each other, although Santos wouldn't admit to it either way—but even if they were police force buddies, he didn't know Kevin Dalton the way she knew him. He could never know Kevin's kindness and good humor and the unrelenting support he had given her when she needed it most.

Much more important than whether Detective Santos believed Cait's story was his revelation that attempted murder charges were being contemplated. Kevin's job was already in jeopardy thanks to the attack, but if he were to be charged with attempted murder, she knew he would likely never work in law enforcement again, regardless of the outcome of a trial.

She was confused and in pain, and now a depression unlike anything she had ever experienced began to weigh her down. She became silent and after a few more fruitless attempts by Detective Santos to convince her to open up went unacknowledged, he pushed away from his desk and smiled his tired middle-aged smile at Cait.

"Something to drink?" he asked.

She shook her head. "How much longer will this take? I'm tired and wrung out and would really like to get some sleep."

Santos gazed at her appraisingly for a moment. "We're almost done," he said.

He walked out of the tiny interview room and a moment later the door opened and Cait was surprised to see not Detective Santos but a woman. She was probably a little younger than Santos, but carried herself with the same world-weary manner. Everyone around here seemed to.

Looking at the new arrival, the thought flashed through Cait's head that hopefully Kevin wouldn't be this beaten-down after a career in law enforcement, and then a tremendous sadness washed over her at the realization he may never work as a cop again.

The woman, Cait discovered, was a police psychologist. She had stringy dishwater brown hair and moist puppy-dog eyes and her clothes were wrinkled, like she had worked a double shift and maybe caught a quick catnap on a couch somewhere.

Her name was Smith. Or perhaps it was Jones, or something equally innocuous. Cait forgot the psychologist's name almost as soon as she gave it and she couldn't find the energy or the interest to clarify.

Dr. Smith or Jones had come to offer support and assistance. Cait didn't care about that, either. All she wanted was to get the hell out of the police station and home to bed, where she could cry herself to sleep and try to figure out what she was going to do next.

Dr. Smith or Jones asked some questions, most of which were remarkably similar to those already asked by Detective Santos. Cait supposed that was by design.

Again she cooperated, although she could tell Smith or Jones wasn't any happier with her responses than Santos had been. Finally she had had enough. She thanked Dr. Smith or Jones for her concern, managing to do so without using the woman's name, and informed her she was leaving. Right now. It had been a long, trying day and she needed to sleep.

Smith or Jones seemed to understand and even enlisted a Tampa cop to drive Cait home. He was a young man, even younger than Kevin, and seemed earnest and pleasant. He tried a couple of times to get her to talk but gave up when it became clear she wasn't interested in conversation.

She issued turns to the young officer as he drove, guiding the cruiser to her apartment building with ease, even though she had never felt so lost in her entire life.

CAIT WAS RELIEVED TO see that the apartment manager had already replaced her front door. Or had fixed it. She wasn't sure which. Didn't care. She could close and lock the damned thing, and that was even more important than usual tonight. Right now it was all that mattered.

She entered her empty apartment, closed the newly repaired door and leaned back against it, exhausted. Suddenly she doubted whether she could even make it to her bed. She slid down, landing in a disheveled heap. Gazed along the hallway floor. From this vantage point it looked smooth and shiny and it occurred to Cait that the building's maintenance man—or someone, maybe the police after photographing the crime scene—had swept up the broken glass and gotten rid of it.

That tiny bit of charity—which in all likelihood wasn't an act of charity at all, but rather an acknowledgement that the glass slivers represented a potential liability issue—was the final straw. Cait buried her face in her hands and the tears came.

She cried for herself, for the horror of being attacked and sliced up by a man with a knife for the second time in less than six months. She cried for the sudden apparent disintegration of the relationship that meant more to her than anything else in the world. She cried for Kevin, lying in a hospital bed, wounded, law enforcement career likely over, possibly facing a charge of attempted murder.

She cried from confusion, and from exhaustion, and from the new-found conviction that her life would never again be normal. She had tried to regain that normalcy after the madness of last summer, had even thought she was making headway, and this was the result.

She cried.

And when she had finished crying, she rose slowly, tiredly, and trudged off to bed.

13

Cait was nervous. Really nervous.

The drive to Tampa's Mercy Hospital was a short one, less than twenty minutes, but she occupied herself the entire way by trying to recall the last time she had felt this jittery and unsure of herself.

Even flying up the East Coast to knock on her mother's door in Revere, Massachusetts last summer, the ultimate cold call, in an attempt to learn her family history—an action she now almost but not quite regretted—had been less nerve-wracking than this. Her first day of work at the law firm had been a breeze in comparison to this.

Then it struck her. She had only been this nervous one other time in her life: before her first date with Kevin Dalton. They had met through a mutual acquaintance, one of those busybody young women constantly fixing eligible singles up with one another, convinced she possessed some mystical insight into the workings of the heart, annoying all her friends in the process.

Cait recalled how she had almost backed out at the last minute. She had been recovering from the end of an unsatisfying relationship, determined not to get involved with anyone for the next few months, especially not a man she had never met, on a blind date set up by a misguided girlfriend with a Cupid complex.

Ultimately, though, thanks to her feelings of guilt at the thought of a last-minute cancellation, she had reluctantly gone through with the date. She remembered being certain it would either be a Titanic-scale disaster or at the very least a long, boring, awkward evening.

It had been neither. The pair hit it off immediately, talking and laughing nonstop, discovering along the way a mutual interest in film noir, literary thrillers, and Italian food. They polished off a bottle of wine, lingering over dessert, finally getting tossed out of the tiny restaurant by a management staff anxious to seat more diners.

Their first date had ended with a chaste kiss on the cheek from Kevin, the evening's only awkward moment and, Cait thought, a charming break from the hordes of young male suitors who seemed to think a two-hour dinner date automatically entitled them to a night of passionate sex.

A second date had followed the next weekend, during which Cait half expected the magic to disappear, that she would discover this handsome, witty, sensitive Tampa cop had a wife or a steady girlfriend, or he was moving to Tibet next week to study under the Dalai Lama. Or that he had experienced an epiphany over the last seven days, discovering he was actually gay.

Or something.

But none of those concerns had materialized. The man who had been handsome, witty and sensitive the previous Friday night remained so. If anything, he seemed even more desirable.

They became exclusive after that second date and were living together six months later, and in the ensuing six years Cait had never once felt threatened or intimidated by the big cop. On the contrary, he was unfailingly gentle and considerate toward her, treating her every single day like he couldn't quite understand how he had gotten so damn lucky.

And that was exactly how Cait felt, too.

Until last night.

She realized she was tearing up again and pursed her lips angrily, forcing back the flood of emotion that was threatening to burst out of her. *Toughen up, dammit. Focus.*

The hospital was by now looming in the distance, a massive, anti-septic-white structure ringed by a series of parking garages that looked like moons orbiting a misshapen planet.

Cait turned into the first garage and took her ticket stub, trying to determine how to approach this meeting. It was something she had been considering since finding herself wide awake this morning at four thirty, scream stuck in her throat, fresh from a nightmare filled with knives and scythes and axe-wielding torturers.

She hadn't been able to fall back to sleep after that and had spent hours considering this very issue, without coming to any resolution. The thought of seeing Kevin was daunting. Intimidating. After years of fitting together with her lover like two pieces of a puzzle, Cait now saw him as foreign, forbidding, unknowable.

It shouldn't be this difficult, she thought as she stepped out of her car and locked the door. *How hard is it to say "Why?"*

HER FIRST THOUGHT WHEN she walked into his hospital room was that she shouldn't have come. It was too painful.

Kevin appeared to be dozing, covered with a thin hospital blanket that rose and fell gently in time with his breathing. An absurdly large swath of bandages covered his right shoulder, where he had been shot by the Tampa cop back in their apartment, and a clear plastic bag filled with some kind of liquid hung from a wheeled stainless steel cart placed next to the bed. As Cait watched, the liquid dripped slowly down a tube, disappearing through a needle into his arm.

His right wrist was handcuffed to the metal rail of the hospital bed. Based on his appearance, pale and wan, Cait thought it an unnecessary precaution, but she had lived with a law enforcement officer long enough to know that procedure dictated just about everything the police did every day, right down to handcuffing a helpless man to his hospital bed if he was in custody.

The cop stationed outside the door had told Cait she would have to hurry, that he wasn't supposed to allow anyone inside the room but was willing to look the other way for a couple of minutes. He also told her to holler if she felt in any danger, a statement that until last night would have struck her as ludicrous.

She felt the time slipping away and wondered if she should even bother to wake him. Maybe this whole trip was a fool's errand. Maybe she should just turn around and leave.

Then he surprised her. She had thought he was sleeping, but into the silence between them he said, "Hey, babe. Come to break me out?"

His voice was weak and strained, but it was unmistakably his own. There was none of the bizarre, robotic tone that had frightened her so badly last night, and Cait's relief was instantaneous and overwhelming. She had intended to keep her distance, at least until she could gauge his mindset, but those intentions were forgotten as she rushed to his bedside, tears welling up in her eyes.

She was beside him in an instant and then she stopped, suddenly unsure of herself, not because she was afraid of him but because she didn't want to hurt him. She had no idea what other injuries he may have suffered besides the gunshot wound.

She smiled and grabbed his hand, squeezing it hard as a tear rolled down her cheek. "I'm so glad you're awake! How are you feeling, are you in any pain?"

"I'm okay," he said, refusing to meet her eyes. "I don't think I could run a marathon at the moment, but something tells me I won't be getting that opportunity for a while." He shook his wrist, rattling the steel handcuff against the stainless steel bed rail for emphasis.

"We'll get this straightened out," Cait said, leaning over his bed and lowering her face until Kevin had no choice but to meet her gaze.

"I'm so sorry," he whispered, his voice barely audible.

"I know," Cait answered. She believed him.

"They're talking about charging me with attempted murder."

"I know."

"I'm not sure that's the sort of thing that can get 'straightened out.'"

"Patience," Cait said. "It looks like it's going to be a while before you're up and around, anyway, so let's take things one step at a time, okay?"

He nodded reluctantly. "Okay. So what's the first step?"

Cait shrugged. It seemed obvious to her. "The first step is to figure out what happened last night." She squeezed his hand again and waited for a response.

Kevin looked up at her, his eyes filled with pain and confusion. "I...I was hoping you could tell me."

Cait bit her lip hard in an attempt to keep from dissolving in tears. Kevin's voice was his own, but his demeanor had changed completely overnight. Gone was the cheerful, self-confident, self-reliant man she had grown to love and to depend on. In his place was a haunted shell of a human being, uncertain and fearful of himself and what he now knew he was capable of.

"You don't remember?" she asked gently.

He shook his head slowly, eyes narrowing, reliving last night as she suspected he'd already done a dozen times. A hundred. "I remember getting home, remember joking about you being there already, about how you're normally not home until much later. After that..."

Cait waited quietly. She didn't want to say or do anything that might take him out of the moment.

"After that," he said again, "it gets hazy. Muddy. Like I was conscious but only barely, like I was seeing things through a long tube filled with clear, thick gel." He furrowed his brow in concentration. "You know how sometimes when you wake up after a dream, you can't really remember anything specific about the dream but you know damn well *something* happened?"

Cait nodded.

"Well, that's what it was like. I wasn't really aware of anything for a few seconds, and then all of a sudden the fog lifted, and I remember walking down the hallway, confused, wondering what I was doing with a knife in my hand, and why there were a bunch of cops in the doorway. And then one of them opened fire and I went down.

"And I remember you screaming," he said, looking ashamed.

Cait stared at Kevin intently. She knew him inside and out. Better than she had ever known anyone in her entire life, maybe better than he knew himself. He was telling the truth. She believed that without question.

And that was terrifying.

Infinitely more terrifying than if he had been lying.

Kevin's entire statement was odd, off somehow, but one part of it was even more bizarre than the rest. "You said the fog—the mental confusion—lasted for a few seconds?"

"That's right."

"Be more specific. How long?"

"I don't know, maybe thirty seconds? Definitely less than a minute."

Cait shook her head. "Honey, you were in that weird fugue-like state for at least fifteen minutes, maybe as long as twenty, before the cops showed up and busted down our door. If one of the neighbors hadn't been spooked by the sound of stuff crashing off our walls and called the police, who knows how long..."

She paused, not wanting to say what she was thinking. "...it would have gone on."

Kevin closed his eyes. When he spoke, his voice was again a whisper, thick with pain. "You mean, who knows how long I would have tortured you."

"No," Cait said firmly. "I don't believe you would have done that. I know you too well; you're not capable of it."

"I took a chunk out of your arm."

"*No!*" she said again. "I know you, you would never hurt me."

They stared at each other, each knowing what the other was thinking.

Kevin opened his mouth to speak but before he could, the door to the hospital room opened and the cop stuck his head inside. "That's long enough," he said. "I could get fired for this. It's time to go." He nodded at Cait and inclined his head toward the hallway.

Kevin said, "Just one more minute? Please?"

The cop sighed. Nodded reluctantly and eased the door closed.

"He's a good guy," Kevin said. "We came up through the ranks together. He's taking a hell of a chance for me. Anyway," he continued, "we only have a second, and I have something to say, so please hear me out."

Cait waited, a sense of alarm rising in her. She thought she knew what he was going to say and didn't want to hear it.

"Until we know what's going on here, I want you to stay away."

"No," she said.

"Listen to me." Kevin's voice was intense. Filled with emotion. "I'm not talking about forever, but for the time being, until we can figure out why...it happened, you're not safe around me."

"*You would never hurt me!*"

"I already did." Kevin nodded at the bandage on Cait's arm and she had no response.

"Stay away," he said again. "I'll be in here for the weekend, probably. My attorney says he's going to try for a bail hearing late Monday afternoon, and if I can make bail, I'll stay in a motel for a while until we can get a handle on everything. You're more important to me than anything else in the world, and I couldn't live with myself if I hurt you again. Or worse."

They stared at each other for a long moment, and this time Cait couldn't stop the tears.

14

The coffee shop was warm and inviting, filled with the typical early morning urgency of people on their way to work. Servers bustled around the small dining room, while the line of customers at the take-out window seemed never to shorten.

The smell of fresh-baked bread and pastries filled the air, a scent Cait normally loved but today barely noticed. She picked at her breakfast, a blueberry muffin, and sipped her coffee, an extra large, and tried to maintain a sense of lawyerly objectivity as she ran the events of the last couple of days over and over in her head while waiting for her guest to arrive.

After visiting Kevin in the hospital yesterday, Cait had driven straight home. She took the elevator to the sixth floor, entered her apartment, and spent the rest of the day behind the locked front door, staring at the blood-soaked fabric of her couch and thinking.

No television. No radio. No books or phone or computer.

Just herself and her thoughts.

And they weren't good. Because no matter how she tried to dissect the situation, no matter how many different angles she examined it from, she could reach only one conclusion.

Milo Cain was involved.

Mr. Midnight. The man responsible for the kidnapping, torture and murder of well over two dozen females—prostitutes, college students and other young women—over the past decade plus.

A remorseless, sociopathic butcher.

Her twin brother.

The problem with her theory, of course, was obvious. Milo Cain was in custody in Massachusetts, comatose and unresponsive thanks to two bullets fired into his head at close range by Caitlyn Connelly herself. The doctors claimed Milo's brain damage was extensive, that there was almost no chance he would ever regain consciousness.

And on the off chance he ever *did* recover, he would still be paralyzed from the neck down. He would then begin the process of standing trial for those murders, for at least two of which the state possessed direct and irrefutable evidence of Cain's commission.

The upshot was that Mr. Midnight would remain incarcerated for the rest of his life and would likely spend every minute of that time in a coma, a lump of human tissue no more aware of his continued existence than were any of the women he had killed.

He could not be involved in the nightmare that was taking place fifteen hundred miles down the coast in Tampa. It simply was not possible.

Still, the similarities between the horror Kevin Dalton had inflicted on her two nights ago—unwittingly, it seemed—and those awful hours Cait, Kevin and her mother had endured in Revere last summer were too obvious to ignore. And Milo Cain, for all his antisocial and psychopathic tendencies, had been extremely intelligent. Probably a genius. If anyone could fool the authorities into believing he was comatose in order to avoid paying for his crimes, it was Milo.

How he might manage it was another matter, but that didn't mean he couldn't.

So Cait's goal this morning was to see if perhaps Virginia Ayers could bring a fresh perspective to the situation. Who better than the woman who had given birth to both of them three decades ago, and who possessed more knowledge about the strange psychic abilities they all shared than anyone else alive?

It was a long shot; there was no question about that. But if nothing else, talking to her birth mother would give Cait a short break from the constant, unrelenting worry about Kevin and what would happen to him, and divert her attention from the fear she might be attacked by a lunatic with a knife—again—at any moment.

And she had no clue what else to do.

WHEN VIRGINIA WALKED through the coffee shop's front door, Cait was taken aback by how frail and ill her mother looked.

Virginia had moved down to Tampa less than two months after the events of last summer, selling the home she had lived in her entire adult life and relocating to Florida. Her aim had been to get close to Cait and Kevin, to make up in some small way for the thirty years she had missed out on when she gave her twins up for illegal adoption within hours of their birth.

It had seemed like the perfect plan. Cait was excited finally to have the opportunity to become close to the woman she had wondered about for so long and had missed so desperately when she was growing up.

But the fact of the matter was that the strain of that long-ago loss of her children, combined with her husband's suicide a few years later and the harrowing ordeal she had suffered at the hands of Milo Cain last summer, had reduced Virginia Ayers to a nearly empty shell of a human being. She had looked far older than her years when Cait first met her six months ago, and her physical decline had only intensified since.

Virginia was in her fifties but could have passed for eighty. She walked slowly, with shuffling, hesitant steps. Her gray skin was wrinkled, her hair limp and lifeless, and although Cait made it a point to see her as often as possible—at least twice a week—her mother's appearance never failed to catch Cait by surprise.

Today was no exception, but with all that had happened over the last thirty-six hours Cait spent little time lamenting Virginia's physical decline. She stood at her small table and waved until Virginia noticed her and began moving slowly across the coffee shop, weaving around customers too wrapped up in themselves to take note of the frail woman walking past.

Cait smiled at her mother and wrapped her arms around her in a careful but enthusiastic hug. She had already ordered Virginia's coffee and the grateful woman slumped into her seat and took a big sip, savoring it for a moment before speaking.

And then Cait felt it.

The sensation of pressure in her head.

It was the same sensation she had experienced just before Pearl Hinton dumped scalding hot coffee on her and the same one she had felt immediately before Kevin attacked her. It was strange, like some invisible person had taken an air hose and begun pumping air into her skull, inflating it like a basketball.

Her hands flew to her head and she gasped. This time, the sensation of pressure was accompanied by a thin line of pain. It was as if the invisible person with the air hose had managed to somehow scratch the inside of her skull with a fingernail.

Virginia put down her coffee and looked at her strangely. "What is it, dear? Is something the matter?"

Cait sat for a moment without answering. The strange sensation had leveled off. The pressure was still there, but as it had done each previous time, it stopped building before becoming unbearable. The pain leveled off as well. She dropped her hands to the table and shook her head slowly, like someone who had awakened from a nap and was trying to clear away the cobwebs. "No, I'm...I'm okay."

Virginia stared a moment longer. Then she took a deep breath and said, "What was that all about?"

"I don't know, exactly. It's...I'm not sure. Have you ever gone swimming and when you toweled off, your ears were blocked up?"

"Not for a long, long time," Virginia answered with a smile. "But I can remember it happening, yes."

"Do you remember how your head felt like it had water sloshing around inside, like whenever anyone talked they were speaking through the other end of a long tube filled with cotton?"

"Sure."

"That's kind of how this feels. It's like a sensation of pressure inside my skull."

Virginia furrowed her brows in concern. "How long has this been going on?"

"Well, that's the thing. It's not constant. It comes and goes. This is the third or fourth time it's happened. It just seems to come out of nowhere, hangs around for a while, and then disappears without warning."

"Maybe you should see a doctor. Have you had it checked out?"

Cait shrugged. "It only started happening very recently."

"Hmm," Virginia said. She seemed to consider this development for a moment and then changed the subject. She clasped Cait's hands in her own and gazed earnestly into her face. "So, how are you holding up, dear?"

Cait had called both her mothers—her adoptive mother as well as Virginia—immediately upon arriving home from the hospital two nights ago, despite the lateness of the hour. She knew middle-of-the-night telephone calls were a parent's worst nightmare, but both women needed to know she was alright before they awoke in the morning and saw the attack reported on the local TV news.

Cait said, "Yes, thank you, I'm doing okay."

Virginia studied Cait's face for a moment and said, "Bullshit. You're not sleeping, are you?""

Cait had known she would not likely fool her mother, and the blunt assessment didn't surprise her, either. Despite her failing health, Virginia Ayers was no shrinking violet. She had lived in a rough-and-tumble, blue-collar city just outside Boston for most of her life, had given her only two children up for adoption when they were just hours old as the only way to save them, and had watched her husband work sixty-hour weeks for most of his life and then end it by hanging himself in a men's bathroom at South Station. She was a tough old bird.

Cait couldn't help smiling at the coarse longshoreman language coming out of the frail little old lady sitting across the table. "No, not really," she admitted.

"Well, I'm not surprised," Virginia said. "Who would expect you to, after what you've been through?"

Then she changed gears again, and asked, "How's Kevin doing?"

Cait shrugged. "He's pretty down, as you might imagine." She filled her mother in on the conversation she had had with him during Cait's brief hospital visit, including his insistence that Cait stay away from him until they could figure out what had happened.

Virginia nodded. "I'm sorry, honey, truly I am. But you didn't call me here to cry on my shoulder, did you."

It was phrased as a statement and for just a moment Cait wondered whether Virginia had received a Flicker from her on the way over here. "Flicker" was Cait's term for the bizarre genetic ability carried in the bloodline that allowed some family members the ability to "see" random events and occurrences from other people's lives. Cait had experienced them since she was a little girl and the occasionally frightening mental images had been prime motivation in her desire to learn her family's history in the first place.

Then she thought about it and realized any mother would have made the same assumption Virginia was making right now.

"No," she said. "I didn't."

"Didn't think so," Virginia said. "And unless I'm way off base, I already have a pretty good idea *why* we're having this conversation. Above and beyond the delicious coffee they serve here, that is. But go ahead. Lay it out for me and I'll let you know if we're on the same wavelength."

Cait paused a moment, trying to decide how to proceed. Finally she sighed and dived headfirst into the pool. "There's something...off...about what happened two nights ago."

"Of course there's something off," Virginia answered immediately. "Your boyfriend tried to kill you, or at least to injure you badly."

"That's not what I mean. You've known Kevin for a few months now, do you honestly, in your heart, believe him capable of the kind of brutal violence he exhibited Friday night?"

"It's hard to know what people are capable of, honey. Sometimes impossible to know. I would never in a million years have imagined your father taking his own life. I knew he was depressed; hell, we both were, from the moment that man dressed all in black strapped you and your brother into the backseat of his car and drove away. It was a depression that never eased. I feel it to this day, and that event occurred three decades ago. So it wasn't like I didn't realize he was hurting. But to kill himself? Your father? I never saw it coming."

Virginia's eyes were distant, haunted, and Cait knew she was reliving the awful moment she found out her husband was dead. She knew also that deep down inside her mother blamed herself for not somehow being able to prevent the loss of life that completed the tragic breakup of her family.

Then Virginia Ayers proved her toughness, snapping out of her self-recrimination and turning a warm smile on Cait, though it was through eyes rimmed in red. "Sorry," she said. "Didn't mean to get off track. But the point is a valuable one—you can never truly know what's inside people's hearts."

"Maybe not entirely," Cait agreed. "But I know Kevin better than I've known anyone in my entire life. I'll admit there are surely facets of his personality he's kept hidden; everyone has them, but to simply snap and try to carve me up? When we had been talking and joking like always, just seconds beforehand? I don't buy it.

"But more to the point," she continued, "the thing that's got me so shaken up is not just the fact that Kevin attacked me, although that's bad enough. The thing that's bothering me more than anything else is *how* he did it. The method he used. A carving knife. Targeting my arm. It was just like..."

She couldn't say it out loud.

Virginia nodded. Her smile was still in place and it was obvious she was trying her best to keep Cait calm.

Good luck with that, Cait thought.

Virginia cleared her throat and nodded and said, "I told you we were on the same wavelength."

"You've considered the similarities?"

Virginia laughed, not unkindly. "Honey, a blind man could see the similarities. I would have to be a blithering idiot not to see them after what happened last summer. But that's not really what you called me here to talk about, either, is it? You really want to talk about what it means."

"Exactly. As hard as it is for me to accept that Kevin could have gone off the deep end and attacked me, at least that's technically possible. But what are the odds he would have chosen *exactly* the method Milo did? It just seems so...unlikely. Impossible, even."

"Maybe seeing it happen made such an impression on him that when he snapped, that was where his mind naturally went."

Cait shook her head vigorously. "No," she said firmly. "He was unconscious when Milo started cutting me, remember? He didn't see a thing."

"But he's heard the story a hundred times since then, has seen the damage to your arm and been by your side as you've gone through the recovery process. It couldn't help but have been nearly as significant an event for him as it was for you."

"I can't argue with any of that," Cait said reluctantly. "But still, the whole thing seems..." She shook her head and felt as though she might break down and cry. Again.

"I know," Virginia said softly. "I feel it, too. It seems your brother *has* to be involved somehow."

"But I thought you said—"

"I've been playing devil's advocate because I want to make sure you're thinking everything through. But you're not the only one who's been obsessing over this whole terrifying mess."

It occurred to Cait out of nowhere that of course her mother would have been deeply affected by the attack on her only daughter, especially given its circumstances. That should have been plain to her all along, but she had been so wrapped up in herself and how *she* had been affected that she hadn't even considered Virginia might be hurting, too.

"Oh, of course you have," she said. "I'm so sorry, I didn't mean to imply—"

"No, honey, you misunderstand. I'm not criticizing you. My point is that after hours of reflection, I came to the same conclusion as you. Milo is involved."

"But how..." The thought hung in the air, unstated but clear to both women. How could a helpless, unconscious Milo Cain, lying in a prison hospital bed fifteen hundred miles away, have orchestrated the vicious attack on his twin, the person he hated more than anyone else in the world? And how could he have managed to do it through Kevin Dalton, a police officer, a young man who had never been anything but utterly devoted to Cait?

"So you don't think I'm crazy?"

"No, honey, I don't think you're crazy."

"Then what's the answer?"

"I wish I knew."

The two women sat for a long time, neither speaking. Cait chewed her muffin and sipped her coffee and thought about the twin brother she had gone thirty years without ever realizing she had. She had learned of his existence and her bizarre family history of twins and murder on the very same weekend last year that he tried to kill her.

And now this.

Cait realized she had a decision to make. She could hang around Tampa and wonder about Milo and how he could engineer traumatic events in her life from all the way up the East Coast.

Or she could travel to Boston and try to get some answers.

And she desperately needed answers.

15

Milo focused hard, trying to clamp down on his rapidly growing sense of panic. It threatened to spiral out of control. The devil-woman suspected his involvement in the assault.

And as much as he appreciated the beautiful irony of Kevin Dalton being reduced to a state so similar to his own—injured and in custody, manacled to a hospital bed—Milo had not expected this development. Why would Caitlyn Connelly's suspicions have gone immediately to him? Why, when his paralysis and coma offered the perfect alibi? Who in their right mind would suspect such a person of assault with a deadly weapon? Who would suspect such a person of *anything?*

The answer to those questions was now clear: Caitlyn Connelly would. Of course. And that was a problem.

Last summer he would have relished the challenge of going head-to-head with The Evil Bitch. Hell, last summer he *had* relished it. The notion of both of them putting their cards on the table and fighting to the death, mano-a-chicko, may the best sibling win, filled him with joy.

But last summer he had been mobile. Last summer he had been able to walk. To run. To drive. To peel skin from the bodies of his victims as if they were nothing more than apples or grapes.

The situation since then had changed, to say the least. Although now in possession of perhaps two of the most significant weapons in human history: the ability to force his will upon unsuspecting others, and the ability literally to experience life through someone else's eyes,

Milo was sufficiently self-aware to recognize that those abilities were offset by a significant disadvantage.

Namely, his utter physical helplessness.

And that was nothing more than a minor inconvenience as long as he remained out of sight and out of mind of his nemesis. She could not cause him problems as long as she remained unaware of him.

But the law of unintended consequences had struck, and at a most inopportune time. The result of his latest unsuccessful attempt to remove her from the planet had represented a change in the status quo, one that could be dangerous—perhaps even deadly—to him were it not managed properly.

Milo took a deep, calming breath, wondering whether the action was all in his mind or whether the rising and falling of his chest was actually more pronounced. He pondered the question for a moment and moved on. It was time to start developing a plan to deal with these developments.

First, the bad news: Milo had brought this problem on himself. The minute he discovered he could transport himself into Caitlyn Connelly's consciousness and *push* suggestions from her mind into the minds of the people around her, he should have had someone kill her and been done with it.

It could have been the law firm secretary. It *should* have been the law firm secretary. Instead of playing around and having the secretary spill coffee on the she-devil, burning her a little but accomplishing nothing in terms of getting her out of the way, he should have forced the woman to kill Connelly once and for all.

The secretary could have strangled her. Or brought the coffeepot into The Evil Bitch's office and brained her with it, then continued smashing her skull until there was nothing left but a ruined pulp and Connelly's blood was leaking out all over the plush carpeting.

There were a thousand ways he could have had the woman dispatch the little bitch, even if the secretary *was* older than dirt. It would have been simple, especially with Connelly being completely unprepared.

But no, Milo had to toy with her. The second he discovered he could push suggestions into people interacting with The Evil Bitch *and watch what happened through her eyes,* he had immediately begun planning something special for her.

Because what could have been more special than using her own lover to send her to the great beyond, and only then after torturing her in exactly the manner Milo had used last summer?

The symmetry was perfect: he would use another man's body to play with her, but would still be able to enjoy it, almost as much as if he were wielding the knife himself. And as an added bonus, the little bitch would know by the very method of her painful death that Milo was responsible.

The opportunity had simply been too good to pass up, and now he was paying the price for his foolishness. Now she suspected him.

But all was not lost.

Caitlyn Connelly's concern that Milo was somehow responsible for Dalton's attack on her, as frightening as that was for Milo, still represented nothing more than unfounded suspicion on her part. Nothing in Connelly's experience—or in anyone's experience—would have prepared her to accept that a comatose and paralyzed Milo Cain could be capable of manipulating someone else's actions from more than a thousand miles away.

And this worked to Milo's advantage.

Suspicions were not the same as convictions, and as long as Milo developed a workable plan and then forced himself to stick to that plan, he should still be able to neutralize Connelly fairly easily. With his superior intelligence and the other advantages he possessed, it shouldn't even be that difficult. She would never see it coming.

The challenge would be to remain under control at all times, to avoid falling victim to the unreasoning fury that overwhelmed him every time he saw—or even thought about—his evil little bitch of a twin sister. Indeed, he could feel the hatred bubbling up in his gut even now, just picturing her, with her beauty and her self-confidence and her disgusting....*goodness.*

It made him want to puke.

He took another deep breath and tried to clear his mind of the clutter. He was smarter than Caitlyn Connelly. He was cleverer than Connelly, more cunning, more resourceful and certainly more relentless. She had bested him once and had escaped his wrath a second time thanks to sheer, dumb luck. She suspected him now but as long as Milo was careful, that suspicion would never translate into anything that could cause him harm.

After a few minutes, Milo could feel himself beginning to relax. The anger and the tension began to clear away and he was able to think. To prepare.

Milo had plenty of faults; he knew that with painful certitude. The very fact that he was lying here trapped inside a useless lump of flesh that was itself imprisoned in a centuries-old stone fortress was proof positive of his failings.

But one thing he was not, and never had been, was stupid. Milo had learned very early in life to take his lumps when necessary and move on. To lose the fight but win the war. Underestimating Caitlyn Connelly had been his worst mistake ever, and then not finishing her off inside her precious law office when he had the chance had been almost as bad.

Fair enough. But the game wasn't over, and he would come back stronger than ever. This time, he would not toy with her.

He would not try to carve her up just to bring himself a moment's fleeting satisfaction.

He would not give her any reason to suspect he was behind her fate, because it wouldn't matter. Who cared whether she realized as she took her last gasping breath that Milo had been behind her death? What difference would that make anyway?

The point was to render her dead so Milo could move on to bigger and better things. And the way to do that would be to make it happen fast, make it look like just another random act of violence, so she wouldn't have even the slightest opportunity to react.

She would never see it coming.

And then he would be rid of her.

Not until that goal had been accomplished would he be able to begin moving forward with everything else he had in mind for the future.

And he had plenty in mind.

16

Cait gripped the armrest tightly as the Boeing 757 floated over the runway at Boston's Logan International Airport. It felt as though the big plane might stay suspended a few feet above the ground forever, or at least until smashing into the triple-decker houses of East Boston that she knew were lurking just outside of airport property.

Then the airliner lurched abruptly downward, striking the pavement and bouncing once before rolling out and beginning to slow. Cait realized she had been holding her breath and released it in an explosive sigh. She had never enjoyed flying but hated it even more now, given the circumstances of the trip and the nagging suspicion that she was abandoning Kevin just when he needed her most.

But she had to be realistic. There was little if anything she could do for him in Florida, especially given his insistence she stay away until he knew for certain that he was no longer a threat to her. What damage he thought he could do while handcuffed to a hospital bed Cait didn't know, but to Kevin the concern was very real. And it seemed obvious to Cait that the key to alleviating his fears would be found here in the frigid February chill of Boston.

Her original plan had been to sneak out of Tampa without telling anyone. She would spend a couple of days in the Northeast and return before either her birth mother or adoptive mother even realized she was gone.

Finagling a couple of days off work had been no problem. Cait had been working like a maniac since last summer, barely taking enough time off to deal with the medical issues resulting from her attack at the hands of Milo Cain. Throwing herself back into her work had been one of the two things that saved Caitlyn—the other being Kevin Dalton, whose quiet strength inspired her even as he dealt with his own recovery—but senior partners at the firm had grown concerned she might be in danger of burning herself out. They had recently gone as far as to strongly suggest she take a little vacation.

The result was that despite its short notice, her trip had been easily arranged.

But that was where her plan of a quick, quiet flight to New England and back had fallen apart. She should have known keeping the trip a secret from Virginia Ayers would be impossible. Roughly two hours after getting her time off approved, the phone had rung, her birth mother bluntly informing her they would be traveling together.

Cait asked, "What makes you think I'm going anywhere?" and Virginia just laughed.

"You're not quite as hard to read as you think you are," Virginia said before extracting a promise from Cait that she would buy two round-trip tickets to Boston instead of one.

Now, as the plane turned off the runway and began trundling along the taxiway to the terminal, Virginia said, "I thought you were going to blow a gasket back there when we were about to touch down. I never knew you hated flying so much. What don't you like about it?"

Cait shrugged. "Good question. I've never really *enjoyed* flying—I certainly wouldn't do it for fun—but this trip was worse than usual. There was some turbulence up there, but even more than the bumpy air, I guess I'm still working through what happened Friday night. And the whole reason for this trip has me a little tense, too. I don't know what to expect, and I hate feeling like I have no control."

"Typical lawyer," Virginia said with a smile. "Always need to be in control."

Cait laughed. "Yeah, I suppose so. But how can you stay so calm and collected considering we have no idea what we're walking into? Or even what we're doing here, really?"

Virginia shrugged. "I don't know. A lifetime of rolling with the punches, maybe. But my feeling is that there's no point worrying about things I can't control."

The plane eased to a stop at the first of a series of long fingers extending from a massive terminal building. Passengers began to stand and collect items from the overhead compartments, even though it might still be several minutes before the exit door opened.

"I wish I could be more like you," Cait said thoughtfully. "I worry about everything."

THE BOSTON HOTEL CAIT had stayed in last summer with Kevin had been clean and comfortable, if not exactly plush. So it was the first place she had decided to check for lodging, and when she discovered rooms were available, Cait had reserved a double for her and Virginia.

The cab ride from Logan was uneventful—at least as uneventful as possible given the reckless abandon with which everyone in this city seemed to approach driving—and now Cait and her mother busied themselves by unpacking their bags and filling the little dresser located at the foot of the two single beds with clothing.

The stay would be a short one, and while she guessed Kevin's inclination would have been to toss their suitcase on top of the writing desk in one corner of the room and remove things as needed, Cait knew her mother would want to get comfortable and the fact was she felt the same way.

The two women worked without speaking. Cait had felt strong and empowered when they left Tampa, as if by coming here she was moving in the right direction, taking action to solve this bizarre problem as opposed to waiting in fear to see what might happen next.

But checking into this hotel, stepping into this room, had changed all that. It reminded her of Kevin, and all she could think about was him lying injured in a hospital room, under armed guard, facing charges he had little chance of defending himself against successfully.

Maybe they should have chosen a different hotel after all. Maybe staying in the place she had shared with Kevin was a bad idea. Picturing him helpless and alone was causing a chain reaction of emotions she didn't need, especially right now. What was she really doing here? What did she hope to accomplish? How could a comatose Milo Cain even bear any responsibility for what had happened?

She sighed and Virginia seemed to sense her despondence. "Hang in there," she said quietly. "You're doing the right thing."

"I hope so," Cait answered, unable to stop her voice from cracking.

Virginia sat on the edge of one of the beds and patted the spread with one hand. "You look exhausted," she said. "You *always* look exhausted lately. We have a couple of hours before dinner, why don't you lie down? Take a short nap. I'll stay right here with you, I'll watch *Oprah* or something, and you can get a little much-needed rest."

Cait couldn't help smiling. She had only known Virginia Ayers for a few months, but she couldn't picture the frail-looking but deceptively tough old bird ever sitting down and watching an entire episode of *Oprah* or any other talk show.

Still, a couple of hours sleep under the watchful eye of her mother sounded wonderful, and she said, "I think that's a great idea. Maybe things will look better when I wake up."

She didn't believe the words even as she was speaking them, but decided to give it a try anyway.

———— ✆ ————

AND IT HELPED.

Sort of.

Cait slept on and off for maybe two hours, aware in some far-off corner of her brain that she was sleeping poorly, tossing and turning and moaning and muttering. Still, she *did* get some rest, and when she finally threw back the covers and sat up in her bed, yawning and rubbing the sleep out of her eyes, Cait had to admit she felt marginally better.

She was still keyed up, worried about Kevin and as unsure as ever about what she hoped to accomplish in Boston. Her stomach was wrapped in knots and she could feel the tension thrumming inside her body like electricity flowing through a high-tension wire.

But at least some of the exhaustion had receded, not really disappearing but fading into the background. For now. Cait had no doubt it was lurking just out of sight, ready to charge back in and take control, but sleep had been a precious commodity the last few days, even more so than usual, and she wasn't about to complain about getting some.

She looked to the right, at the identical double bed next to hers with an ancient nightstand placed in between. Virginia returned her gaze steadily, her eyes clear and bright despite her otherwise feeble appearance.

Cait ran her hands through her tangled hair in a fruitless attempt to straighten it a little. "Did you get any sleep?" she asked.

"I didn't try," her mother said. "I wasn't tired."

Cait nodded in the direction of the television, which Virginia had apparently never turned on. "Couldn't find *Oprah?*"

"I lied about watching her," Virginia said without a trace of embarrassment. "I can't stand that windbag."

Cait laughed. "So what did you do while I was sleeping?"

"I watched over you."

"Wasn't that a little...I don't know...boring?"

"Quite the contrary, honey. I lost you when you were less than twenty-four hours old, missed out on three decades with you. I never saw your first steps, never watched you lose your first tooth. No piano lessons, no first dates, no graduations. I missed out on so much, and the worst part was the knowledge that I would never get to know you.

"When you came back into my life, it was the most frightened I had ever been. The reason we were forced to break up our family in the first place was the knowledge of the awful history of twins in this bloodline. The history of murder. If we had raised the both of you, you would never have survived; Milo was destined to kill you. Hundreds of years of bloodshed had proven that point beyond any doubt.

"But when I saw you standing at my front door that day last summer, in addition to being the most terrifying moment of my life, it was also the happiest. Seeing the beautiful and successful young woman you've become has made every second of heartache worthwhile. I'm so fortunate to have gotten to know you, so fortunate you're finally back in my life. And now that I've gotten that second chance, I want to make the most of every single minute we have together. Sitting with you while you sleep is about as far from boring as it could possibly be for me."

Tears welled up in Virginia's eyes as she talked, and Cait realized with some surprise that she had begun crying as well. She thought back to the first three decades of her life, to all the nights she cried herself to sleep wondering what was wrong with her, why her own mother had considered her so worthless and damaged as to be beyond even attempting to save.

She knew now that as much as she had suffered over those thirty years, the toll on Virginia had been far worse. Giving up both her children just hours after their birth, questioning herself daily about the wisdom of her decision for years after, seeing her husband succumb to the unending numbness in his soul and take his own life, and then finding her daughter years later only to discover her son had become one of the most notorious serial killers in the history of the United States, all of it had aged her far beyond her years.

It had sapped her vitality.

It had practically killed her.

And yet here she sat with Cait, accompanying her on what would undoubtedly prove to be the wildest of wild-goose chases, not just uncomplaining but actually happy to be here.

It made Cait realize that as unfortunate as she had thought she was for all those years, she was that lucky and more now. She swiped at her eyes with a sleeve and sniffled. "I love you, too," she said simply. "Now let's figure out how we're going to get to the bottom of what's going on here."

MILO CAIN LAY MOTIONLESS in his empty room. He was always motionless, and his room was nearly always empty, the only exception being those few minutes every day when a nursing crew would bustle in, changing linens, bathing him, refreshing his colostomy bag and changing his clothes.

Milo hated those few minutes and every day spent them counting the seconds, impatient for them to be over. Fortunately, given his status as a reviled and feared sociopath, the nurses were none too anxious to hang around—it was as if they feared his illness might be contagious—and they hurried through their tasks as quickly as possible, gossiping and chatting as they worked, but wasting no time on *this* particular chore.

They had, of course, no idea Milo could hear and understand them, although he doubted it would have made any difference if they had. And he didn't care either way.

The nurses and guards didn't matter. All that mattered was that they do what they had to do and go away, leaving him alone to think. And to plan, which was what he was doing now.

The room was cool and quiet. Empty. And Milo was lost in thought, trying to calculate the best time to slip back inside Caitlyn

Connelly's head and begin to put his plan in motion. Doing so would come with a cost, he now knew. He would suffer extreme exhaustion, and it would grow significantly worse the longer he stayed inside her.

It was a price well worth paying, but it was important he plan properly, so as to get the most bang for his buck. So to speak.

So he considered. And he calculated. He knew The Evil Bitch was planning to fly up here to New England. What the hell she thought she might accomplish by doing so was beyond him, but Milo realized that was irrelevant. He was unable to push suggestions into his twin sister's consciousness, so he couldn't stop her from coming, and *that* was the relevant factor.

She was coming.

And given the fact that he knew she was coming, he tried to estimate when she might get here. That was critical, because when she arrived, he planned on finishing her off once and for all.

For a while he had considered doing it while she was still in Tampa, but with lover boy Kevin Dalton in custody she now lived alone for the time being, and there was no real way of knowing when she might be around other people. Popping into her skull while she was in her apartment packing for her trip would do him no good and would just waste effort for no good reason. Same thing if he entered her head while she was driving to the airport. Unless someone else was in the car with her, he would be helpless to hurt her.

But once she arrived in Boston, there would be people around her almost constantly. She wasn't coming all the way up the coast just to sit alone in a hotel room, so as long as he didn't jump into her head very early in the morning or very late in the evening, he knew he had an excellent chance of catching her around other people.

People he could use to kill her.

And that was what he needed.

The problem was that the concept of time for someone trapped comatose inside his own body was much different than for a normal person, who could gauge the passage of it easily by glancing at a clock, or by observing the sun rising or setting, or in any of a hundred other ways.

Milo didn't have that luxury. But he *did* have the daily nurse's visits, which he had determined almost always occurred around mid-afternoon. That being the case, he guessed it now to be late afternoon. He felt confident Connelly would not have wasted any time booking a flight to Boston once she had made her mind up to come, so she had probably already arrived in the city.

All of these calculations meant that the odds were good she would be out in public, most likely either sitting down to dinner in a restaurant or in a cab on her way to eat. If he was wrong, and she was alone when he popped into her head, he would simply stay for a short time, try to get the lay of the land and some idea when she would no longer be alone, then exit quickly and wait for a better opportunity.

But he didn't think he was wrong.

He was hardly ever wrong.

17

The Crow's Nest Grill and Tavern was located on the waterfront in downtown Boston, just north of the New England Aquarium. Despite its rather pedestrian-sounding name, The Crow's Nest was home to what the locals almost universally acknowledged as the finest and freshest seafood available, and in a town like Boston, that was saying something.

Virginia hadn't eaten at The Crow's Nest in ages. Even in the years before Robert's suicide, money had been tight; afterward, making ends meet was a continual struggle, and dining out at any restaurant that didn't feature a drive-through window along the side of the building wouldn't have been feasible financially even if she had wanted to, which she didn't.

But Cait's trip to New England last summer hadn't included much sightseeing—they had been far too busy trying to stay alive to play tourist—and this time Virginia was determined to give her daughter at least a small taste of life in the Northeast.

Besides, her concern for Cait's wellbeing was growing almost by the minute. With all that had happened, the poor girl looked on the verge of a nervous breakdown. The formerly hard-charging, self-confident lawyer was pale and drawn, with dark circles under her eyes and a defeated stoop to her shoulders.

She had been beaten down and she needed a few hours to do nothing but relax. They would have dinner and a couple of drinks, then hopefully get a good night's sleep and be ready for tomorrow.

At the door, a smiling young man greeted them. He was dressed in old-time seafarer's garb, or at least what Virginia assumed was meant to be old-time seafarer's garb. The restaurant was brightly lit, clean and busy, and the young man led them to a table not far from a massive plate-glass window facing the open water of the Atlantic Ocean.

"Have you dined with us before?" the man asked, pulling Virginia's chair out for her and then doing the same for Cait's.

"Not in more than thirty years," Virginia answered.

"Then you're in for a treat. During the warm weather, our outdoor patio is available for dining. This time of year, obviously it's a bit too chilly for that, so you'll have to make do with an indoor experience. Still, people have been enjoying The Crow's Nest for nearly fifty years, in all weather conditions."

He waited for them to get settled and then said, "Your server will be along in a moment. Please, if you need anything, don't hesitate to ask, and have a wonderful evening." Then he was off.

The view was spectacular, and Virginia was treated to the sight of Cait's eyes widening in awe as she took in the panorama. Darkness was falling but a little daylight remained, steel-gray as a result of solidly overcast skies. The Atlantic looked turbulent, threatening.

"It's...wonderful," Cait exclaimed.

Virginia laughed and said, "You've lived in Tampa your entire life, haven't you?"

Cait nodded, her eyes still fixed on the view outside the big window.

"Well, you must have seen the ocean thousands of times, then."

She shook her head. "Not like this. The Gulf Coast can be stormy, obviously, but there the waters look tropical and inviting most of the time. This is different. It looks forbidding, like we're being warned away."

"Well," Virginia said, "that friendly young man just informed us The Crow's Nest has been here for almost a half century, so I think we'll be safe enough from Mother Nature's wrath while we're here."

Cait dragged her gaze reluctantly away from the picture window and mumbled, "It's not Mother Nature I'm worried about."

Virginia watched her daughter, saying nothing, staring steadily until Cait was forced to glance up at her. "Let's not forget why we're here," she said quietly. "We didn't fly fifteen hundred miles just to eat fresh clam chowder and lobsters and enjoy the view, as wonderful as it is. We're going to hash out a game plan."

"I know," Cait said. She seemed to make a conscious effort to relax. "But sometimes it seems so hopeless. As horrible as that day was last summer inside your house, I thought we had turned a corner, and things were going to be...I don't know...*normal*. Whatever that means."

A bubbly young woman brought menus and took their drink orders and then bounced away. Virginia waited until she was gone and said, "One thing I learned a long time ago is that life will never be normal for those of us in this bloodline, at least where twins are concerned. I've researched our family history exhaustively, both online and through hard copies of birth records, etc., going back hundreds of years in some cases."

"And?" Cait had picked up her menu and Virginia thought she was scanning it for dinner choices, but when Virginia looked across the table, her daughter's intense blue eyes were above the menu top, locked onto her.

"And most of what I've learned you already know. Twin births have been prevalent throughout our history, much more so than in the general population by a factor of ten to twenty times. And in every case I could find, those twin births were followed by the murder of one by the other, sometimes in their youth, sometimes in adulthood, but always, without exception, in a gruesome manner."

Cait was watching her without speaking. Virginia took a deep breath and continued. "Now, where the births were *not* twins, the children seem to have developed normally and grown into typical adults, with the exception of the ability you're so familiar with, the ability to see Flickers.

"But it's probably not realistic to expect your life ever to be normal, honey, at least not as the term 'normal' is generally understood. But that doesn't mean you can't have a happy, fulfilling life."

"It does until people stop trying to kill me." She lowered the menu and gazed with haunted eyes at Virginia. "I keep going back and forth about Milo being responsible. It just seems so unlikely, but it's the only explanation I can come up with for what Kevin did to me. His actions Friday night were brutal, and he's simply not a brutal man. He's never been anything but kind and gentle and accommodating to me since the day we met."

The waitress returned and Virginia ordered for both of them. Cait was so distracted Virginia doubted she would be able to handle the simple task, and she knew what Cait would like, anyway: lobster dinner with a side of New England clam chowder.

As the waitress disappeared into the kitchen with their order, Virginia took a moment to consider how to proceed. Then she said, "Lots of people given up for adoption choose to investigate their roots when they get older, so the fact that you did so isn't unusual. But in your case there was another reason as well, wasn't there?"

Cait didn't answer. Virginia had turned her attention to the massive picture window—the magnificent ocean view really was hypnotic—and now she looked back at her daughter. Cait's hands framed her head as if she was experiencing the onset of a migraine.

"What is it?" Virginia asked.

"It's...I don't know...nothing, I guess. You remember I told you about that sensation of pressure I've been experiencing on and off inside my head?"

Virginia nodded without speaking.

"It's back," Cait said. "And this time it was accompanied by a sharp pain, like an invisible spike was being driven into my skull. The same thing happened last time but it wasn't quite as intense. This one was more painful and lasted longer."

Virginia furrowed her forehead and glanced around the dining room. It was a reflexive action, and she wasn't even sure why she did it. What did she think she was going to see?

Everything seemed perfectly normal inside the restaurant and after a moment she refocused on her daughter. "Are you all right? Do you need a doctor?"

"I guess I'm okay," Cait said after a moment. "I don't think I need a doctor; I don't even know what a doctor could do, anyway. The pain's gone but the feeling of pressure is still there. It's very strange."

"When we get back to Tampa, you'll need to make an appointment."

"Yeah, maybe. I guess so."

"There's no guessing involved. You're doing it," Virginia said firmly. "Maybe I missed the first thirty years of your life, but I'm your mother and you're going to take care of yourself."

"Fine," Cait said reluctantly. "Fair enough. Now, what were you saying?"

Virginia glanced around the restaurant again and then said, "I was mentioning that while many people given up for adoption try to uncover their roots when they get older, you had more of a motivation than most, didn't you?"

"You know I did," Cait answered immediately, shaking her head slowly. It was obvious she was still bothered by the odd sensation inside her skull. "I wanted to find out if I was the only one in the world who could experience those little mental movies in my head, those snippets of other people's lives I called Flickers, or whether that ability was shared by others in my family tree."

"Exactly," Virginia said. "That's perfectly natural. And in addition to discovering you had a twin brother, you learned what?"

"I learned that you had experienced Flickers your whole life, as had many in my bloodline, and I learned the things about twins that you just mentioned. It was much more than I ever expected to discover."

Virginia nodded in encouragement. "I know it's hard for you to go back to that afternoon when Milo invaded my home, but think about that for a moment. How did we get out of that horrible situation again?"

"You already know how," she said, a flash of irritation showing in her eyes.

"Humor me," Virginia said. "Let's work through this. There's a point to the exercise, I promise."

Cait sighed. "Okay. We got out of it because Milo had kicked your pistol under the couch when he first forced his way inside your house. In the chaos that followed, he forgot all about it. I was able to grab it after I had fallen partway off the couch while he was...slicing the skin off my arm. I...I picked it up and I shot him with it."

Tears rimmed her daughter's eyes, her head was down and her breathing had turned ragged.

Virginia hated taking Cait back to that awful day, but Cait's therapist had said talking it through would eventually allow the young woman to work past what had happened. To move forward with her life. Eventually.

But in this case, there was another reason as well. Virginia persisted: "And how did you know that gun was under the couch? It was mine, not yours, and you had never seen it. You didn't even know I owned a gun."

"I knew because..." Her voice trailed away and then she raised her head and looked into Virginia's eyes. She was suddenly sharp, focused. "I knew because you *pushed* that knowledge into my head. You had been trying to do so the entire afternoon, but I was so focused on Milo, and on Kevin's injuries, and the fact he might be dying, that I resisted it. I didn't allow the information in until I was so weakened and distracted I couldn't stop it."

"That's right," Virginia said. "This ability to push suggestions into someone else's head was something you had never experienced, isn't that right?"

"Never. I was totally unaware of it. In fact, I've *still* never been able to do it."

"Most of the time I can't, either. I couldn't tell you why I was able to do it that day. Maybe it was luck; maybe divine providence, maybe it was brought on by the stress. I don't know. But the point is..."

"The point is that there are aspects of this...ability...that I may not be aware of. That neither one of us may be aware of."

Virginia smiled. During their conversation, Cait's eyes had regained some of their usual intensity. A little color returned to her face and she sat up straighter in her chair, her body language conveying strength and determination now, whereas before she had looked defeated. Hopeless.

Cait continued. "So," she said, thinking out loud, "the fact that we don't know how Milo could be involved in Kevin's attack on me really doesn't mean anything. He might be manifesting some ability we simply aren't aware of."

Virginia nodded, still smiling. "Exactly. That's not to say he *is* involved, only that we definitely can't eliminate it as a possibility. And now that we're here in New England, we just have to figure out a way to determine the answer to that question."

18

Milo watched through Caitlyn Connelly's eyes with a growing sense of anger.

Indignation.

The lack of respect being afforded him by the people who should have been closer to him than anyone else in the world, people related to him by blood, was shocking. It was a betrayal that more than justified every bit of what he had attempted to do last summer.

And it didn't surprise him, either. Not at all. Very few people possessed the intellectual capacity to truly fathom him and his motives. He was more highly evolved than most—including his blood relatives, obviously—so being misunderstood came with the territory.

But to see it so clearly, to watch the betrayal real-time through the eyes of the main conspirator, was beyond maddening. That, combined with the unavoidable hatred he felt every time he saw or even thought about his twin sister was enough to make his blood boil.

Even though he had vowed not to lose his temper, Milo could feel his control beginning to slip. He wanted to cut and slash, to make that arrogant little bitch and her mother bleed, to watch them suffer, to stab and slice and peel the skin away from their worthless bones while they screamed for mercy, but he would offer no mercy, why should he offer mercy of any kind when they were sitting and conspiring against him, he would do no such thing, he would simply continue cutting and stabbing and slashing until—

No.

Milo forced himself to stop.

He would not fall victim to the unreasoning rage, justifiable though it was, brought on by the sight or the thought of Connelly. He was better than she. Quicker- witted. Smarter. Cleverer.

The effort required to bring himself back from the brink was superhuman. It was beyond what he had ever believed himself capable of. But he managed it. He had nearly fallen into the black chasm of rage, but had stopped himself, a fact of which he was proud. It was one more example—if he needed any more, which he didn't—of his advanced state of evolution.

Milo took a deep breath and centered himself, choking back his natural revulsion at being connected to the person he despised more than anyone else in the world. He had entered her head to execute a plan, and that was exactly what he intended to do.

When he was done, he would never have to worry about The Evil Bitch again.

He watched dispassionately through her eyes, taking in the surroundings, trying to determine where in the hell they were as he waited for the right moment to strike. It was obviously a restaurant/lounge, obviously in Boston or the immediate surrounding area, but Milo recognized nothing about it.

He knew he had never eaten there. Unsurprising, he supposed, given the fact that his pockets had rarely contained more than a couple hundred dollars at any one time. This place was upscale, right on the waterfront, not the sort of eating establishment typically frequented by people like him—the homeless, the displaced, the mentally ill.

No matter. Milo kept his simmering anger in check as Caitlyn Connelly and their mother—their *mother!*—dissected the horrible Milo Cain, analyzing the monster's every perceived fault in painful detail. He forced himself to get past the character assassination and focus on the restaurant's surroundings, because that was what mattered. That was why he was here.

The tables were arranged in no particular pattern that he could discern. It was like a giant had lifted the roof off the building and tossed a bunch of tables inside and wherever they landed was where they had stayed. Waitressed scurried about, carrying trays of food and drinks through a swinging door to the right and then down a narrow corridor and into the dining room.

On the other side of the restaurant was a bar, and that was where Milo focused his attention. The bar represented the best chance to put his plan in motion.

The lighting was dimmer inside the bar than in the dining area, but with every glance Connelly took in that direction, Milo could see the setup was perfect. A roughly four-foot-high half-wall separated the dining room from the bar, meaning he could see its interior—or at least everything above the half-wall, which was all he cared about anyway.

The tables inside the bar were scattered about in the same seemingly random manner as those in the dining room. All of the tables were occupied, and all by parties of at least two people. Milo ignored them.

A half-dozen or so drinkers were bellied up to the bar, all of them men, ranging in age from late twenties to maybe early fifties. Every time Connelly flicked her gaze in that direction, Milo focused on these men. They were the key.

This was taking too long. Milo knew that. He needed to finish up here and get out of Connelly's head or risk suffering the extreme exhaustion—ironically, given his situation, the coma-like symptoms—that he experienced before.

Still, the time was right, and the setup was right, so Milo stayed, waiting impatiently for his chance. The problem was that Connelly was engaged in such a serious fucking conversation with Mommy Dearest that most of the time her attention was devoted to the dried-up old biddy seated across the table from her. Only rarely did her gaze shift to the rest of the dining room.

Eventually, though, after what seemed like forever, Milo selected his mark. A middle-aged man, forty-five years old or so, unremarkable-looking. Forgettable. The sort of guy who could walk through a crowded room and go unnoticed by everyone.

The sort of guy Milo Cain used to be.

When he could walk.

When he could move.

When he was conscious.

After settling on the man, Milo waited for Connelly to glance into the bar one more time. It took a few minutes, but when she did, he *pushed* a suggestion, through her, directed at Mr. Unremarkable.

The man at the bar twitched noticeably, like he had just received a small electric shock, and then he froze for a moment. He turned away from the bar. Took one big glassy-eyed step toward the open doorway separating the bar from the dining room.

Then Connelly's attention shifted back to her mother and Milo lost sight of the man. But Milo had seen enough to know his suggestion had been implanted. He smiled. He had planned to exit Connelly's consciousness at this point, but he just couldn't bring himself to leave when things were about to get...good.

So he stayed in Connelly's head. He promised himself he would jump away soon, certainly before she died. He wasn't any closer to knowing what would happen if he was still in her head when she croaked than he had been last Friday, and he had no intention of finding out the hard way.

But he wanted at least to see the beginning of the action.

19

Matt Coyle rarely spent time in places like The Crow's Nest. He had never eaten here before, and after fifteen years as a Boston police officer, the last seven spent in the Drug Control Unit, he would have bet a hundred bucks that he had chowed down at every last eatery the city had to offer, at least the ones that didn't insist on suits and ties as a prerequisite for entry.

Matt was more comfortable inside the many dive bars and strip clubs typically favored by Boston's drug-trade entrepreneurs than the higher-end establishments catering to casually dressed businesspeople and tourists. Much more of his work was done in those places.

But tonight was not a typical night. Tonight, instead of rousting dealers dressed in gang colors, wearing sideways baseball caps and mirrored sunglasses, with baggy jeans sagging off skinny asses, Matt was hoping to come one giant step closer to taking down a major player.

He had spent months working to establish a connection inside Boston's financial district, where the drug trade was known to be rampant, and carried high hopes into tonight's meeting. A high-rolling, mid-thirties wheeler-dealer at one of the city's major brokerage firms, hopelessly addicted, dead-ass broke and with the wrong people knocking on his door in the middle of the night, had agreed to meet Matt and discuss the possibility of trading information—name, dates and other specifics—for immunity from prosecution and protection from the bad guys.

It was the opportunity of a lifetime as far as Matt Coyle was concerned, a potential career-maker, the sort of break that, if handled properly, could lead eventually to awards, publicity, promotions and maybe even high-paying private sector security gigs.

Eventually. If handled properly.

Right now, though, Matt was determined to keep his eye on the ball and stay focused. His potential informant, a slickly dressed weasel Matt had taken an instant dislike to, originally requested to meet at the Four Seasons, a proposal Matt nixed without negotiation. There was no way his bosses would pay for dinner at one of the ritziest—not to mention priciest—dining establishments in town, and Matt wasn't about to pay out of his own pocket, career-maker or not.

Plus, he had an almost pathological aversion to suits and ties, without which he wouldn't have been allowed through the door at the Four Seasons. He was in the driver's seat and he knew it, so his counterproposal had been The Crow's Nest, one hell of a nice place as far as Matt was concerned, and a restaurant that would not break the bank, either.

The informant's name was Stan Crafowski, and he sat across the table taking full advantage of the free meal and drinks. Given that Crafowski probably made more money in a week than Matt earned in a year, this went right up Matt's ass, but he chalked up the aggravation to the cost of doing business.

The potential informant reminded Matt of the stereotypical used-car dealer, oozing the oily charm and easy patter people associated with rip-off artists. In the back of his mind, Matt wondered how anyone could trust this guy with their life's savings or their retirement accounts.

"So, Stan," he said. Crafowski had insisted on drinks and then a full dinner before discussing business, and the greasy bastard's plate was now nearly empty.

Close enough, Matt thought, and continued. "You know what I bring to the table—full immunity from prosecution and your safety guaranteed by the Boston police for as long as you provide us with actionable information and your sworn testimony when the time comes. It's a pretty good deal the way I see it."

"Yeah, I guess so," Crafowski said, somewhat reluctantly. He was jittery and sweaty despite the fact the temperature inside The Crow's Nest was cool and comfortable. *Heroin.* He looked to Matt like he was in serious need of a fix, and Matt guessed this would be a short meeting.

He decided to push hard before Crafowski got cold feet or so dopesick he bolted from the restaurant. "You don't need to guess. Take it from me; it's a good deal. It's certainly the best you're going to get. So let's get down to brass tacks. What do you have for me? And I want specifics, something I can act on immediately and get results to show my bosses, to prove to them that dealing with you will be worth their considerable trouble and expense."

Crafowski took a deep breath, shoveled in another bit of food, and began describing a fellow broker, supposedly his drug connection as well as the dealer for dozens of other young, addicted professionals in Boston's financial district.

As he talked, Matt glanced around the restaurant, making his boredom apparent. He had decided against taking notes, recognizing that to begin scribbling specifics on a notepad in the middle of dinner would be the surest possible way to guarantee his informant would clam up. Instead, he had gotten Crafowski to agree to have his statement recorded.

That particular arrangement had been negotiated last week, when this meeting was being set up, and Matt suspected the strung-out little bastard had probably forgotten all about it by now. But that was his problem. Crafowski's signature was on a release, all legal and binding, and that was good enough for Matt.

The tiny voice-activated recorder was nestled in the breast pocket of Matt's dress shirt, saving every last word for posterity. His boredom act was a put-on designed to elicit diarrhea of the mouth from the informant. Matt had long ago discovered that if people thought you weren't paying attention, they tended to volunteer a lot more information.

So he gazed around the restaurant and his eyes fell on a drunk stumbling out of the bar. It was still early, just past eight p.m., but this dude must have started drinking the minute his shift ended, because he was toasted. His eyes were glassy, his movements slow and lumbering.

Matt hoped the guy was either planning to walk home or call a cab, because getting behind the wheel right now would be a monumentally stupid decision. Had he not been in the middle of one of the most important meetings of his career, Matt might have been tempted to tell Crafowski to hold his thought—his rambling, drug-addled thought—and have a quick word with the drunk, maybe personally call him a cab. Matt had overdone the drinks himself on occasion and been on the receiving end of similar kindness from more than one stranger.

He stayed seated, though, and made just enough eye contact with Crafowski to keep the guy talking. If half of what the financial planner was saying was true, Matt thought he might be on the verge of one of the biggest drug busts the city had ever seen.

His eyes wandered back to the drunk. The man was middle-aged, maybe ten years older than Matt, dressed casually but conservatively. Just a regular guy.

But after leaving the bar area, the drunk did something unexpected. Instead of turning left, toward The Crow's Nest's front entrance, he turned right. Matt thought maybe he was heading to the men's restroom but remembered there was only one.

And it was in the other direction.

He began to get an uneasy feeling in the pit of his stomach. Matt Coyle had been a cop a long time and that feeling was like radar, a sixth sense that veteran law enforcement officers tended to develop after years spent dealing with trouble day in and day out.

Something was wrong; he was certain of it, although he had no clue what that something might be.

The man walked/shuffled/staggered forward and Matt had the absurd thought that the guy looked like an extra from the movie *Zombieland.*

He sat up straighter in his chair and paid even less attention to Stan Crafowski, who hadn't noticed anything amiss and who continued to vomit information like there was no tomorrow. Now that he had started speaking, it seemed he had no intention of stopping until he had given up everyone in Boston's financial community.

Matt barely noticed.

The drunk seemed to have zeroed in on a table for two located across the room. A pretty young lady, maybe a few years younger than Matt, shared the table with an older woman who was clearly her mother. They were spitting images of each other. The two women were engrossed in an intense conversation and thus far had not noticed the man's bizarre actions.

The drunk moved toward the two women as straight as an arrow—or as straight as possible, given the funky configuration of the dining room and his extreme inebriation. He banged against tables and spilled drinks and bounced off patrons. They bitched and complained but he paid them no attention.

Matt started rising from his chair. Maybe the guy was an ex-husband or former boyfriend who had been sulking about a bad breakup, drinking himself into oblivion when his ex happened to walk into the restaurant and now he was planning to...Matt didn't know what the guy might be planning to do, but he was certain it would not be good.

Crafowski noticed Matt getting to his feet and stared at him in jittery junkie surprise. "What's..." he started to say but Matt ignored him and he shut his mouth.

Matt's eyes focused on the drunk. The man had by now almost arrived at the table where the two ladies were dining. The younger woman finally spotted the guy and her eyes grew wide, whether with fear or recognition Matt didn't know. Maybe both.

Matt picked up the pace, moving to intercept the man and lead him out of the restaurant, by force if necessary, when the man surprised him again. An empty longneck bottle of Budweiser sat on top of the table next to the ladies, and the man plucked it up with his right hand, a surprisingly adept move for someone who had been staggering across the dining room so awkwardly.

Then without taking his eyes off the pretty young lady, the drunk swiveled his wrist and smashed the beer bottle against the edge of the table. It shattered, stopping conversation in the dining room like someone had flipped a switch.

A split second of perfect silence was followed by a single scream from across the room. Then another patron joined in and chaos erupted. People scrambled away from the drunk, spilling out of their chairs and scrabbling across the floor in a mad rush toward the exit. A waitress dropped a tray of food and it fell with a clatter, dishes shattering and food and drinks spilling, splattering the legs of those closest to her.

And Matt broke into a sprint, shoving aside frightened diners heading the opposite direction like spawning salmon swimming against the tide. The drunk lifted the shattered beer bottle, now half its previous size, its brown glass spiked with deadly glittering shards.

He lifted his arm and slashed at the young woman's neck. She threw herself backward in her chair with the reaction of an elite athlete, and the weapon whizzed past her neck, somehow missing her entirely. Matt wouldn't have thought it possible.

But the woman was going to be helpless and exposed, unable to defend herself. Her body flew backward and she landed in a heap on the floor as the drunk stumbled, off-balance from his wild lunge. He banged into the table and the older woman bravely stood and slapped him hard across the face.

She was older, though, and weak, clearly ill, and the blow bounced off the drunk like a pebble clanging off a large boulder. The drunk reared back and shoved the overmatched elderly lady with his free hand, apparently saving the broken beer bottle for the younger woman.

The older lady flew backward and smashed into the wall, sliding down it and crumpling to the floor. The drunk paid her no more attention. Instead, he turned toward the young woman. She struggled to get clear of the chair she had fallen onto and tried to scramble backward and away from the threat.

But there was nowhere to go. She made it maybe three feet before smashing into another of the restaurant's tables and a now-empty chair. The man lifted the beer bottle high, above his shoulder, and leaned forward, bringing the bottle forward and down at the young woman, again aiming for her neck or throat.

And Matt launched himself.

He dived headfirst over a table, leaving his feet and driving his two-hundred-pound frame at the glassy-eyed drunk, who was still so focused on his deadly attack he was utterly unaware of Matt Coyle hurtling at him from his blind side.

Matt wasn't going to make it. He had been too slow.

Suspended in the air, Matt watched as the razor-edged bottle slashed toward the woman. At the last possible moment, she shoved hard with her feet, spinning sideways, and the bottle ripped through the left sleeve of her blouse, biting into her upper arm but missing her throat.

Blood gushed from the injury and the bottle impacted the floor, and then Matt crashed into the drunk. He body-slammed the man and they tumbled, the force of the tackle driving them both into the side wall. They crashed to a stop next to the older lady, who was just beginning to push herself shakily to her feet.

"Boston police. You're under arrest," Matt said, breathing heavily. The broken beer bottle had fallen to the floor next to them and he kicked it away. Then he flipped the drunk onto his belly and yanked the man's hands roughly behind him. He had no cuffs so he simply leaned a knee heavily into the man's back, between his shoulder blades, and waited for the cavalry to arrive.

It wouldn't be long. In the distance he could already hear sirens shrieking. A middle-aged man in a tie with a nameplate pinned to his breast pocket—the restaurant manager, Matt assumed—bent over the younger woman, tending to her injuries, while a small crowd gathered around the older woman and helped her to her feet.

Matt glanced back toward his own table and cursed. Stan Crafowski was nowhere to be seen.

20

"I've never seen the man before," Cait said to the cop who had saved her life. She sat perched on the edge of a hospital emergency room bed as a young ER doctor finished bandaging her upper arm.

The gash opened up by the broken bottle had required more than twenty stitches to close, and although Cait began to wonder if there would be one square inch left undamaged on her arms by her next birthday, she considered herself extremely lucky. The bottle had missed her throat by inches.

"You're sure about that," the cop said, not asking a question. It was clear by the tone of his voice he didn't believe her.

"I'm sure," Cait repeated. "I live in Tampa, I've only been to this area once, last summer, and when I was here, I never had any interaction with that man. I would have remembered."

"There must have been something," the cop said. The cop's name was Matt Coyle and he reminded Cait so much of Kevin it made her heart ache. Roughly the same age, they shared the same soulful, expressive eyes, earnest demeanor and obvious goodness.

Cait shrugged and looked helplessly at the young cop.

"Listen," he said, sitting next to her as the doctor finished his work. The wax paper covering the bed crinkled under his weight. "The suspect, the man who attacked you with a broken bottle, is named Drew Houghton. Mr. Houghton is forty-three years old, married with two young children, and has never been in trouble in his life. Never been arrested. Never been charged with a crime. He got a parking ticket once. As far as we can determine, that's the extent of his criminal history. He's an average guy.

"Now, Mr. Houghton is facing a charge of attempted murder," the cop continued. "Ms. Connelly, I've been a police officer a long time, and I can tell you it doesn't work that way. Law-abiding citizens just don't get up one morning and decide to murder an innocent woman they've never met."

"I understand," Cait said, "but that doesn't change the fact that I've never met the man or, as far as I know, ever interacted with him or even seen him until today. I know you'd like to hear otherwise but it's just not the case."

The cop sighed. "Don't misunderstand me, Ms. Connelly, I'm not blaming the victim, nothing like that, I'm just trying to understand what happened."

"You and me both," she said.

Changing tactics, he said, "So what are you and your mother doing in Boston?"

Cait wanted to tell him the truth. *I have no idea. I don't know what I'm trying to accomplish with this trip, but I have a strong suspicion that what happened tonight is related to it somehow.*

Instead she said, "I'm just here to see my...brother."

"Really. And who's your brother?"

Cait kicked herself for her honesty. Why couldn't she be a better liar? She took a deep breath and continued. She knew exactly how the conversation would go from here. "My brother is Milo Cain."

The young cop opened his mouth to speak and actually got a couple of syllables out. "And wha—"

Then he stopped, jaw hanging open, and fell silent. A second went by, and then two, and then five. The cop closed his mouth and his eyes narrowed and he said, "I knew I recognized you from somewhere.

You're the woman held hostage over in Revere last summer. You..." His voice trailed off.

Cait smiled wearily. "That's me. We were held inside my mother's house. She's since moved to Tampa to be closer to me."

The cop nodded absently. "I remember the whole thing now," he said. "I know one of the guys who busted down the door of that house. Not well, but a little."

He was silent for a moment and then said, "There has to be a connection."

"What do you mean?"

"On your first trip ever to the Boston area you're nearly killed by a notorious serial murderer who happens to be your brother, and then on your second trip, you're almost murdered again. No one is that unlucky, Ms. Connelly."

She debated telling this cop, with the earnest demeanor and the kind eyes, the truth. Almost did. But then she realized she didn't know what the hell the truth *was,* and if she started spouting nonsense about Flickers and comatose suspects, all of her suspicions entirely unsupported from a law enforcement standpoint, she would come off looking not just unbelievable, but downright loony.

So she dropped her eyes and said, "Apparently I am. I've never seen that man before."

The cop ran a hand through his hair. Cait could see he was frustrated. "Ms. Connelly, I was in that restaurant as part of an investigation I've been working on for months. I was there to meet a confidential informant. In all the excitement, the man disappeared and I don't know if he'll ever talk to me again. A whole investigation, potentially down the drain. And it was all worth it. I wouldn't change a thing. Honestly. But please help me out here."

"Officer Coyle, I'm not trying to be ungrateful. I'm incredibly appreciative of what you did and I'm well aware of just how lucky I was tonight. You saved my life and I'll be indebted to you forever for that.

But I simply don't know why that man might have attacked me. Maybe he just snapped. I'm being completely honest with you, though, when I tell you I've never met him before."

Cait could see the man knew he had gotten everything he was going to get out of her. He nodded as if to himself and handed her a card. "I know there's more to this than what you're telling me," he said. "I just can't figure out whether your silence is because you don't *know* the connection between the two attacks or because you just don't want to say. But there's something there. If you decide you want to tell me what it is, any time of the day or night, please call me. My precinct number is on there, as is my personal cell number. Use it."

Cait took the card and pocketed it without looking at it. She was tired and sore and had never felt so hopeless in her entire life.

"I will. And thank you."

21

Milo could barely control his rage. Once again his best-laid plans had fallen apart through no fault of his own.

He had leapt out of Connelly's head just as the useful idiot from the bar was driving the broken beer bottle down at her throat. There was no way anything could go wrong. She was cornered, helpless and her panic was obvious.

Although exhausted from the length of time he had spent inside Connelly's head, Milo had forced himself to stay awake afterward. He waited a few minutes and then, with an extreme effort of will, tried pushing himself into the old biddy's head. That was how badly he wanted to see The Evil Bitch lying dead on the floor with blood spurting out of her neck and pooling on the floor around her.

He knew Virginia Ayers was his biological mother and supposed he should have felt some attachment to her, some kinship, but there was nothing. It wasn't surprising, though. Milo felt no attachment to his adoptive mother, either, she was just some bitch who had bossed him around when he was a kid until he had gotten old enough to beat feet and disappear, which was exactly what he had done.

But still, as a member of his bloodline, and a possessor of the unusual ability his family seemed to share, Milo suspected he would be able to inhabit Virginia's consciousness, just as he had discovered, entirely by accident, that he could inhabit Caitlyn Connelly's.

And it worked.

He insinuated himself into the old bat's head, sliding right in and seeing through her eyes, exactly as he had been able to see through Connelly's. He could hardly contain his excitement. Once satisfying his need for proof that The Evil Bitch Connelly was really gone, he could take his time moving forward, rest and recover and develop a game plan.

The Evil Bitch was the only one who could hurt him. Virginia Ayers might have her suspicions about him—obviously she did, in fact, based on what he had seen through Connelly's eyes at the restaurant before the attack—but she was irrelevant. She was old and frail and tired, beaten down by life.

The old broad would never pose a danger to him, and besides, he didn't want to kill her too unless it became absolutely necessary. It was kind of nice having a portal to the outside world, even if his perspective was limited to whatever his unwitting host happened to be experiencing at the time of his "visit."

But once inside Ayers's head, when he took his first look through her old, rheumy eyes, the shock had been overwhelming. Almost too much to take.

Impossibly, Connelly was alive.

She was still fucking alive.

Even worse, with the exception of what looked like a decent gash to her arm, she was unhurt.

Some interfering busybody had managed to stop Milo's useful idiot before he was able to do any real damage. Milo was stunned and angry, confused. He had stayed inside Connelly's head for absolutely as long as he dared, and things had been moving along perfectly and according to plan.

This was impossible.

And yet there was the evidence, staring him—or more accurately, staring Virginia Ayers—in the face. The busybody knelt on the attacker's back, keeping him secured until help could arrive, while some other busybody tended to the still very much alive Caitlyn Connelly.

He watched in shock and disbelief for a few more seconds and then jumped out of the old biddy's head.

And raged.

And ranted.

For one of the first times since discovering his awe-inspiring ability, Milo wished he could move. He wanted to lash out, to slash things and kick things and break them. To set fire to something. To destroy and kill.

He was like a little boy, lost in a temper tantrum, aware it was accomplishing nothing but unable to stop himself.

His anger was justified. No one would have been able to contain his disappointment after once being again denied the way Milo had been. He was only human, after all, even if his version of humanity had evolved far beyond everyone else's.

After a few minutes spent out of control inside his own head, the white-hot flame of Milo's fury began to burn itself out, replaced by a bone-tired weariness he had never before experienced.

He was exhausted, even more so than the last time.

Had he been able to move, he knew he would *not* have been able to move.

Just before sinking beneath the waves of his own exhaustion, a single thought ran through Milo Cain's feverish mind: *This isn't over. Not by a long shot.*

22

The alarm went off at eight a.m., buzzing in Cait's ear like a bee-hive. She opened an eye blearily and felt around with one hand, slapping at the offending clock, unable to remember how to turn the damned thing off. Eventually the buzzing stopped, but by then the damage was done. There would be no getting back to sleep.

She rolled onto her back and closed her eyes. The newly sutured gash in her left arm throbbed with the bright intensity of a fresh wound. The partially healed burn on her right forearm alternated between an irritating feeling of extreme sensitivity and an itch that no amount of light scratching would vanquish.

And she had a headache.

She lay quietly for a moment, taking stock. The injuries were bad enough, but by now she had become used to dealing with a certain amount of physical pain. The headache was what concerned her the most. The headache was different. Something very odd was happening to her—the bizarre cranial pressure that seemed to come and go at random intervals, each occurrence accompanied by a bolt of extreme pain—and Cait's initial fear was that this morning's headache might signal the onset of another bout of that frightening sensation.

It was the last thing she needed. She was nearly at the end of her rope. But after a moment of reflection, eyes closed, head resting on her pillow, Cait decided this morning's headache was exactly that: a headache. Nothing more, nothing less.

She could live with that.

She rolled onto her side and opened her eyes to see her mother gazing back at her. Virginia looked wide-awake and alert, and Cait said, "Good morning. You were awake before the alarm went off, weren't you?"

Virginia smiled and said, "I told you I value every minute I get to spend with my long-lost daughter. Why would I waste any of my time sleeping?"

"I hope you spent at least *some* of it sleeping!"

Virginia winked at her but said nothing.

Cait yawned. "Remind we why we decided eight o'clock was a good time to get up?"

"Go back to sleep, honey. We can get a later start than planned; it won't hurt anything."

"Nah," Cait said. "That was more of a rhetorical question than anything else. I'm fully awake now. Besides"—she took another look at the cheap digital clock on the hotel's nightstand—"we have to be at the hospital in less than two hours."

"We could reschedule. Milo's not going anywhere."

"No. I don't want to reschedule." At the mention of her twin brother's name, Cait felt a wave of despair wash over her, black and heavy, and she knew she was in for another long day. No surprise there. She was getting used to them.

She sighed and climbed out of bed, feeling exhausted. "And I wouldn't be so sure about your last statement," she added.

THEIR DESTINATION WAS the town of Bridgewater, located roughly thirty-five miles south of Boston. The two women walked out of the hotel at eight thirty, having showered, dressed, packed their bags and checked out, and Cait asked Virginia, "What are we going to do when we get there? We're probably going to be close to an hour early."

She had asked the question in all seriousness, but her mother seemed to find it amusing. "What's so funny?" she said.

"Honey, it's obvious you didn't grow up around here. The way the traffic is in the Boston area, we're just as likely to be late as early."

An hour and fifteen minutes later, the massive Bridgewater State Hospital structure loomed in the windshield of their cab, appearing completely out of place in suburban Boston. Its dark brick and stone construction had the forbidding look of a medieval castle, but instead of being surrounded by a moat, the complex featured a double chain link fence topped by a snarl of intimidating razor wire.

As they approached, Cait could see a series of guard towers spaced at even intervals between the fences. Security cameras were everywhere. The scene served to remind approaching visitors that, regardless of the facility's name, they would not be entering a typical hospital. It was a correctional facility, and its "patients" were some of the most danger-ous and frightening men to be incarcerated in the Commonwealth of Massachusetts.

The cab eased through a wheeled gate that was currently open but could be rolled across the entryway at a moment's notice, undoubtedly at the touch of a button by the officer manning a security booth just in-side the hospital grounds.

At the booth, the driver rolled to a stop at a lowered wooden se-curity bar and buzzed down his window. A moment later a uniformed guard stepped out of the booth and approached, his face dour-looking and suspicious. "Help you?" he said.

Cait lowered her own window and said, "Good morning, Officer. We're here to see one of your...uh...patients."

The man was silent for a moment, his face impassive, as if she had spoken a foreign language and he was trying to translate her words. Fi-nally he said, "Visiting hours don't start until three thirty."

"I understand, but we have an appointment. It was set up through the warden's office."

"Wait here." The guard turned around and stalked into the security booth without waiting for a response. A moment later he returned holding a clipboard. He bent down to get a good look at the two passengers in the backseat of the cab. "Names?"

"Cait Connelly and Virginia Ayers."

"I'll need to see some ID."

The women fished out their driver's licenses and passed them through the open window and the man disappeared again, returning after a short delay and handing them back.

"Go to administration," the officer said to the driver. "It's straight ahead, at the end of the circular drive." He looked into the backseat and continued. "When you get to administration, you'll have to check in and pass through the metal detector. The admin folks will help you from there."

Then the guard turned around and reentered the small security building. A moment later, the heavy security bar in front of the cab lifted and the vehicle accelerated onto the prison grounds.

They were in.

Cait felt as though she could barely breathe.

THE INTERIOR OF THE one-hundred-fifty-year-old structure was as drab as the exterior. Decades-old linoleum tile covered the floors, its finish long since worn away, the coloring faded and indistinct. The walls featured puke-green paint badly in need of a touch-up, and ancient doors creaked to an ill-fitting close behind Cait and Virginia as they were escorted to the warden's office.

The trip through the metal detector had been uneventful. Cait had researched Bridgewater State Hospital online prior to the visit and had read stories—apparently inaccurate—of mandated strip-searches and lengthy questioning of visitors.

They encountered none of that, although security was tight. Guards were uniformly tight-lipped and somber, exactly as the man at the gate had been. Cait had, of course, read news reports of the unexpected and violent suicide of Bridgewater's previous warden—while locked inside his office at the hospital—and she assumed that horrific occurrence had much to do with the atmosphere of brooding negativity.

Or maybe the place was like this all the time.

At the warden's office, their armed escort ushered them inside a small, marginally more pleasant suite. "I'll leave you in the competent hands of the warden's administrative assistant, Ms. Bickford," the man said.

Then he turned to the older woman—her hair had been tinted a vague blue and Cait had to stifle a smile at the sight—and said, "Give me a call when they're finished here and someone will be back to escort them to the prisoner's room."

Then the guard was gone. The elderly lady looked more like a retired librarian than the assistant to the warden at one of the most dangerous correctional facilities in Massachusetts. She was all business, though, and said, "Please take a seat. Warden Pend–"

She caught her mistake and paused a moment. "I'm sorry," she said quietly. "I worked a long time with Warden Pender and it's very hard to get used to the notion that he's gone."

"It's no problem," Virginia said kindly before Cait could answer. The look on her mother's face told Cait to step back and let her do the talking, which Cait had no problem with. She was still feeling vaguely hazy and unsure of herself. "You were the one who found the warden, weren't you?"

"Yes, I was," the woman said reluctantly. "It was one of the worst days of my life." Tears filled her eyes and she dabbed at them with a tissue she had been holding, apparently for just this purpose.

"Had Warden Pender been depressed prior to his...death?"

"Why do you care about that?" the secretary said sharply.

Virginia raised her hands in a soothing gesture and kept her voice low. "No reason," she said, although Cait suspected that was not the case. "I apologize for upsetting you."

The woman nodded curtly and lifted her right hand, tissue still clutched inside it. She pointed at a bank of uncomfortable-looking chairs lining one wall—to Cait they looked exactly like a row of prisoners lined up for execution, but maybe it was just the setting—and said, "Please take a seat and I'll let Warden Ciuffetti know you're here."

"YOU UNDERSTAND MILO Cain is comatose and completely unresponsive to all stimuli." It turned out Warden Ciuffetti was a woman. She was dressed in a long gray wool skirt, a tan silk blouse, and low-heeled shoes. She had pulled her hair into the tightest bun Cait had ever seen and everything about her demeanor screamed "severe." She reminded Cait of Nurse Ratched from the old Jack Nicholson movie *One Flew Over the Cuckoo's Nest.*

Cait waited for Virginia to answer and when she didn't, said, "Yes, we understand." Apparently her mother's need to talk had been satisfied by her brief conversation with the emotional Ms. Bickford.

The warden waited a beat and then spread her hands in a gesture of confusion. "Then why..."

Cait shrugged. "I just needed to see"—she hesitated and gulped air—"my brother." The words tasted bitter in her mouth.

"You just needed to see him."

"That's right."

Nurse Ratched drummed her fingers on her desk. A stain that looked a little like dried blood covered a large portion of the desktop. It had clearly been scrubbed and sanded, but no amount of scrubbing would ever eliminate all the evidence of the tragedy that had taken place on its surface. "You flew all the way from Tampa to see your paralyzed, comatose, incarcerated brother on a whim."

Cait pursed her lips. "I wouldn't categorize it as a 'whim,' but I'll admit to the decision being relatively spur of the moment."

"After not laying eyes on him for more than six months."

She felt a stab of annoyance, and like clockwork her attorney persona kicked in. It felt oddly satisfying to be back on territory she understood, even if the sensation was only temporary.

"This visit was prearranged and preapproved," she said. "In fact, I was told to arrive *before* the start of regular inmate visiting hours, so as not to upset the other visitors by exercising my right to see the notorious serial killer Milo Cain. I was told not to breathe a word to the media. I was told if I showed up here accompanied by a camera crew or any media representative, I would not be permitted on hospital grounds. I have honored all of your requests fully.

"Now, after jumping through your hoops, I find myself undergoing some kind of interrogation. I don't appreciate being treated like a criminal, Warden"—she craned her neck to read the woman's name off a prison ID hanging from a lanyard around her neck—"Ciuffetti. I don't appreciate it one little bit. What's the problem?"

The warden sat back in her chair. It was easily as old as the stained desk and it creaked with the motion as if lodging a complaint. Nurse Ratched's angular face conveyed tightness and anger, but after a moment she spoke, keeping her voice neutral.

"There's no problem," she said. "However, you must understand things have been strained and security's been even tighter than usual around here since Warden Pender's suicide. The warden was a generous, outgoing, friendly man—I knew him personally and professionally for over thirty years—and he never once exhibited any of the signs one would expect to see in a person contemplating taking his own life."

Cait nodded, prepared to accept what seemed to be meant as an apology, but the woman continued to talk. "There has even been speculation that the warden was murdered, despite being found in an office locked from the inside and having received no visitors that morning."

The new warden blinked and shook her head. Her angular face now looked pinched, like she had just bitten into spoiled meat. "*I* don't share that view, of course. The physical evidence was clear, and it all pointed to only one thing: suicide. It's just that the way it happened was so..."

"How did it happen?" Cait asked softly.

"He sawed through his own throat with a letter opener."

Cait couldn't help reacting. She swiveled her head to look at Virginia and discovered her mother was staring back at her. It was obvious they shared the same thought: *Milo*. The use of a sharp-edged tool to maim and kill could not possibly be coincidence.

Could it?

If the warden noticed their shared glance, she made no mention of it. "Anyway," she said, blowing out a breath. "I apologize for giving you the third degree. It's just that the timing of this unusual visit, coming right on the heels of Warden Pender's bizarre death, caught me a bit by surprise. I wouldn't want to see you or anyone else hurt."

"I understand," Cait said, although she didn't.

Warden Ciuffetti pressed a button on the old-fashioned console telephone on one corner of her desk. "Have Officer Caldwell escort Inmate Cain's visitors to his hospital room now, please."

THE CONFIDENCE THAT had come from pushing back against the warden leached out of Cait almost immediately. It was replaced by a bleak foreboding that she realized had been steadily building from the moment their plane touched down in Boston.

The feeling of hopelessness continued to grow as they wound their way through a maze of dusty and mostly empty corridors. Officer Caldwell was not the same guard who had escorted her and Virginia to the warden's office upon their arrival, but he was no more talkative and no friendlier than the first.

Cait wasn't sure what she had expected Bridgewater State Hospital to be like, but this wasn't it. The place seemed uniformly silent, almost as if it were empty except for them. There were no shouted curses from inmates, no banging on cell bars. Hell, as far as Cait could see, there *were* no cell bars to bang on. Only an endless array of winding corridors and office doors, all closed and, presumably, locked.

We must be in an administrative wing, she thought, wondering what all of these empty offices might be used for. The silent guard continued to lead them along dimly lit corridors and through locked double doors, stopping each time they arrived at a set and waiting to be buzzed through by other unseen guards monitoring their progress on an endless array of CCTV cameras.

At the end of a long hallway they moved through one last set of doors and then down a stairway, arriving at what looked more like a hospital, circa the 1950s, than the prison cellblock Cait had been expecting. Then it occurred to her: of course Milo would be in a hospital room and not a cell; he was paralyzed and in a coma.

Officer Caldwell—Cait had dubbed him *Silent Cal* in her head—led them down another long corridor. This one was filled with closed doors, just like the administrative wing, but on the other side of these doors were hospital rooms, most of them empty.

At the end of the corridor, Silent Cal gestured to a closed door on the right and said, "This is Inmate Cain's room." The disdain in his voice was obvious, and Cait assumed he had meant for it to be. "I'll be right outside the door if you need me."

"Thank you," Cait said, her voice sounding small and insignificant, seeming to struggle into the dense Bridgewater State Hospital air and vanish. Her heart was racing and she felt jumpy and afraid. If she could have managed it without getting lost, she thought she might have sprinted outside to the cab, which was waiting in front of the complex with their luggage.

She glanced at her mother. Virginia seemed unruffled. She still looked frail and ill, but Cait thought she could have passed for a woman strolling through the neighborhood grocery store rather than waiting to be allowed inside the room of one of the worst mass murderers in the history of Massachusetts.

Cait paused at the door, assuming it would be locked like all the others had been. Officer Caldwell stood six feet behind them in the hallway examining his fingernails, making clear through his posture he had no intention of putting forth one ounce more effort than the absolute minimum required of him.

She reached out and turned the handle and to her surprise the door opened. She turned to Virginia, who offered a small smile of encouragement, and then entered Milo Cain's room.

A GRIMY WINDOW, TOO small to accommodate even the tiniest of human beings, sat high on the far wall. Despite its miniature size, the window was covered with steel mesh on both sides and a set of iron bars. As a result, only a minimal amount of daylight was able to fight its way inside, and the room was dim almost to the point of darkness.

And it was practically bare. No curtains adorned the little window. A single plain wooden bureau stood against one wall, its top bare. A bedside table, as plain and unadorned as the bureau, was the only other furniture in the room.

Against the wall to her left a standard-looking hospital bed jutted out into the middle of the small room like an extended middle finger. Lying in the bed, covered with a single ratty prison blanket, was Milo Cain.

The notorious murderer.

Her nemesis.

Her brother.

He lay unmoving, of course; eyes closed, of course. Cait hadn't seen him since that terrible afternoon inside Virginia's tract house in Revere last summer, not once, and he looked much smaller than she remembered. What she could see of his muscles appeared shriveled and atrophied.

He looked helpless.

But still, as she ran her eyes over his prone form, she could barely breathe. She felt herself being transported back to the day she thought she was going to die. No, that wasn't quite true. It was the day she *knew* she was going to die, her skin peeled away from her bones by Milo Cain.

The bile rose in her throat and she began to hyperventilate. Turned to leave, to run, she didn't care where, just to get out. She had to get out.

She took two blind steps toward the door and then felt a calming hand on her arm.

She looked up, panicked and afraid, and saw Virginia next to her, as unruffled as ever. Her mother smiled reassuringly at Cait, who stopped moving. Stopped everything. Forced herself to breathe. Felt her pulse beginning to slow to normal.

This is just a room, she told herself, *no different than any other room in the hospital portion of this castle of the damned.* A monster occupied the room; that much was true. But the monster was helpless. He lay unseeing and unfeeling before her, no more of a danger to her or anyone else in his current state than was the plain wooden dresser shoved up against the wall.

She breathed deeply, her mother still stroking her arm. Willed herself to relax. And began to see Virginia Ayers in an entirely new light.

Her mother was more than just a frail woman, old before her time, who had endured so much tragedy and loss; more than anyone should have to endure in a single lifetime. Virginia was more impressive than Cait had ever imagined, possessing reserves of strength she could only marvel at.

It occurred to Cait that no matter what she accomplished in her life she would never be as strong as her mother.

Slightly more relaxed, she turned her attention to the still form of her brother. He of course hadn't moved, and wouldn't until someone came along and moved him.

"He doesn't even seem like the same person," she whispered to her mother, who was rapidly becoming her rock.

"You don't need to whisper, honey," she said. "He can't hear you."

Cait wasn't so sure about that.

She had never been one to put stock in the concept of "evil." Oh, she knew it existed, had experienced it firsthand to a horrifying degree last summer, but she had always believed the terrible things that human beings were capable of doing to one another were nothing more than the result of choices made by those individuals.

But now, standing just a few feet away from the man who had damaged her so badly, Cait could sense a corruption emanating from the broken body of Milo Cain, a rot that struck her as spiritual just as much as physical. It was as if a black cloud hung over the hospital bed to which her twin was chained, and that cloud was filled with maggots, squirming and wriggling, struggling to break free and wreak havoc and destruction.

She felt the fear rising again from deep within and reached for her mother's hand. Virginia took it and squeezed, seeming to understand everything Cait was feeling. It occurred to Cait that her mother probably was going through everything she was, maybe even to a greater extent. After all, Milo Cain was her only son, the son she had given up under the most difficult of circumstances more than thirty years ago, the son who had then grown up to become one of the most reviled and feared men in American history: Mr. Midnight.

Cait glanced at Virginia. She remained totally composed. A little paler than usual, perhaps, but otherwise none the worse for wear especially compared to Cait, who felt as though she might fall apart at any moment.

"Why are we here?" she said to her mother.

"We're here to exorcise demons," Virginia answered. "And to prove to ourselves once and for all that this man, for all the damage he's done and all the heartache he's caused, can't hurt us anymore. Can't hurt us ever again."

"Then why do I feel like we're in as much danger right now as we were last summer?"

23

Milo could hear them. His "mother" and his "sister." They were standing in *his* room talking about him as if he weren't even there.

It was infuriating.

Milo considered himself lucky to even be aware of their presence. The disaster at The Crow's Nest last night had so totally exhausted him that he had dropped off into unconsciousness, ironically placing him in the comatose state everyone already thought he had been in since getting shot in the face last summer.

But just a few minutes ago he had awoken, snapping instantly alert to the sound of Virginia Ayers and Caitlyn Connelly discussing his many faults and weaknesses in hushed tones at his bedside.

If he weren't afflicted with paralysis, Milo's entire body would have been trembling in fury at their utter unmitigated gall. First they manage to escape him last night, through the intervention of some random asshole, and now they come to his home, to his own territory, to rub his nose in his failure?

It was more than infuriating. But it strengthened his resolve. He had sworn to eliminate the stain of Caitlyn Connelly from the earth and that was what he would do. He had failed twice, but he wasn't finished yet. Not even close. And he only needed to succeed once.

As he listened to the two women disparage him, unable to move a muscle or even open his eyes, Milo cursed his bad luck yet again.

They were alone. He knew they were alone not just because he could hear no other voices inside his room, but because he could sense the presence of no one else. If another person had been standing in his room *besides* Virginia and The Evil Bitch, he would have known; he was sure of it.

And that was a shame. Because if even one other person had been present, Milo could have jumped into either Virginia's or Connelly's head and pushed a suggestion into the third person's brain. He could have taken another whack at her right this minute, and eliminated his problem at last. Finally.

It was especially galling because Milo knew there was a guard here somewhere. There had to be. Milo had been a resident of Bridgewater State for months now and he knew that no one, not even the warden of this medieval shithole, ever entered his room without at least one guard in the immediate area.

In the beginning, after being transferred here from the *real* hospital, it had been a team of guards, at least three and sometimes four, who accompanied visitors, as if maybe he was somehow fooling everyone with the paralysis and coma schtick, and was just waiting for the right moment to open his eyes, magically remove the handcuffs that kept his unresponsive body chained to his bed rail, and leap to the floor, attacking everyone like a madman.

The whole charade had been fucking ridiculous. And there were a lot of visitors in the beginning, too. Lawyers, and psychologists, and reporters, and medical professionals, and more lawyers, all coming supposedly for legitimate purposes, but what they really wanted, Milo knew, was to gawk at the helpless serial killer, rendered powerless by his evil bitch of a twin sister, all of them thinking he could hear nothing they said when in reality he heard everything. Every last word.

But that had been in the beginning. Over time, the flood of visitors became a trickle, eventually drying up entirely, when the novelty of Milo Cain wore off and some other shiny trinket captured the public's attention. The contingent of guards accompanying those visitors had been trimmed from three or four back to two, and then eventually one.

And whereas in the beginning the guards had surrounded his bed like a pack of wolves stalking a wounded deer, after a while it got to the point where they didn't even come inside the room anymore on the rare occasions Milo received a visitor.

Which was exactly the case today.

And even though the guard was outside the door, his location wouldn't prevent Milo from pushing a suggestion to kill Caitlyn Connelly. The problem was that without knowing which guard was out there, he had no way of knowing which head to push the suggestion into. He could only push one suggestion at a time, and this prison had dozens of guards running around. They were like fucking cockroaches.

So he had no choice. Milo lay there and listened to the infuriating chirping of the two people he hated more than anyone else in the world. And that was saying something.

But this is not over, he kept reminding himself. *This is not over.*

24

"So, what do you think?" Caitlyn had been deep in thought, staring out the window of the cab as it carried them back to Logan Airport and their flight out of Boston and back to sanity. Her mother's question caught her by surprise and she jumped, startled. She was embarrassed by her reaction but unable to prevent it.

She thought about the question and then shrugged. "He's as helpless as a baby. Heck, he's *more* helpless than a baby, because at least a baby can alert others to its needs by crying. Milo is nothing more than a big lump of inanimate tissue, technically alive, I suppose, because he continues to breathe and his heart is beating."

Virginia nodded and said nothing, and Cait continued. "But he is *completely helpless*. There is absolutely no way he could be influencing even the things that occur inside his own hospital room, much less events happening fifteen hundred miles away in Tampa."

"So, do you feel better?"

"No. Not at all. In fact, I feel much worse. Something is very wrong here. Something inexplicable is happening, and the circumstances of that warden's suicide are a perfect indication of that. The method he used is so...similar...to Milo's preferred method of torture and murder, and so...similar...to what was done to me by Kevin last week, that I just can't accept the notion that the whole thing is just coincidence."

Virginia seemed unsurprised by her words. "So, what do you think is going on?"

"I think you know. Or at least suspect."

"What do you mean?"

"You said it before: back in Revere last summer, you *pushed* the location of your gun into my head somehow. It saved my life. But you also said you think Milo may have somehow picked up the ability to push suggestions into people's brains. Somehow Milo has learned to bend those unsuspecting victims to his will and force them to do his bidding."

"But Milo's in a coma. He's unconscious and unresponsive. He can't hear anything. How could he be doing any of what you say?"

By now Cait realized her mother was again playing devil's advocate, forcing her to think the issue through and confront the reality of what was happening in a way she had not been able—or even ready—to do before. Now the answer to her mother's question came to her like a bolt of lightning out of a muggy summer sky. It was so obvious she couldn't believe she hadn't seen it before.

"He's in there somewhere," she said wonderingly. "He's not *faking* anything, he actually is comatose, but even though his physical state is unresponsive, somewhere inside his brain the old Milo Cain is still there. And still aware. And he's using that awareness to push suggestions into people's heads in order to continue wreaking havoc and destruction."

The scenery flashed by, the Yellow Cab driving much too fast for Cait's Florida sensibilities, but barely keeping pace with the other Massachusetts traffic. Cait was glad her mother had chosen this moment to bring up the subject of their discussion. It kept her from focusing too closely on the possibility of their suffering a violent death in some gruesome traffic accident. And wouldn't *that* be ironic.

"You've already figured this out, haven't you?" Cait said.

"I wouldn't say I've figured anything out exactly, but I've had my suspicions about this, as you already know, almost from the moment I learned the specifics of Kevin's attack on you."

Cait felt like a blind woman whose eyes had been opened and could see clearly for the first time in her life. "Something else has been bothering me as well," she said after a moment of silence.

Her mother raised one eyebrow and waited for her to continue.

"Just before that man attacked me with the beer bottle inside The Crow's Nest last night, I had another one of those episodes that have been coming and going recently."

"The sensation of pressure inside your head. I remember."

"That's right. It happened as we were talking, just before all hell broke loose. It couldn't have been more than two or three minutes later when that man came out of nowhere and tried to slice my throat."

Virginia shrugged. Cait noticed that her mother's eyes bored in on her with an intensity that nearly seemed to match her gaze that afternoon six months ago inside her house, when she had desperately sent the mental message that allowed Cait to stop Milo Cain from skinning her alive. That obvious intensity gave lie to the feigned indifference of the shrug.

"Coincidence," she said, her eyes never leaving Cait's.

"I don't think so," Cait answered, shaking her head slowly. "I've given this a lot of thought. The first time I can remember feeling that sensation was just before Pearl Hinton scalded my arm with the hot coffee in my office. The next time was later Friday night, just prior to Kevin going crazy. Last night it happened right before some random guy I'm one hundred percent certain I've never met tried to kill me by slicing my throat open with broken glass."

As she spoke, her eyes left her mother's face and wandered back to the cab's side window, where the scenery continued to flash by. Now she returned her gaze to her mother's face as an unreasoning terror began to fill her. It eclipsed anything she had ever felt, even greater than what she had experienced when Milo Cain was busily peeling the skin off her forearm.

Because if she was right, she had absolutely no control over anything.

"It's Milo," she whispered. "Milo is somehow entering my head, isn't he?"

Virginia was silent for a moment. Then she said, "We don't know that for sure."

"But it's what you think, isn't it?"

"Yes," she said simply. "I wasn't convinced until this last incident, but when you said last night while we were sitting at the table inside The Crow's Nest that the pressure sensation had returned, I immediately felt that you might be in danger."

"I noticed at the time that you seemed to become very tense for no particular reason. Then all hell broke loose."

Virginia nodded. "It was my fault," she said. "When nothing happened right after you mentioned the pressure in your head, I let my guard down. If I hadn't, I might have seen the man coming…"

"It wouldn't have made any difference," Cait said. "There was nowhere to go, nothing you could have done."

Virginia shook her head. "I'm so sorry," she said, "about all of this. If I had been stronger last summer and stood up to Milo instead of calling you back to Revere as you were getting ready to fly to Florida, you'd still be safe and none of this would have—"

"No." Cait reached across the cab's backseat and squeezed her mother's hand. "Don't be sorry," she said. "Finding you was the best thing that's ever happened in my life. I don't have a single regret."

But that didn't mean there wasn't any fear. Cait tried to keep herself under control. She felt as though the fear building up inside might just be too much for her body to contain and she would explode like an overinflated child's balloon.

She tried to ignore the implications of her theory about Milo Cain but could not. If he somehow possessed the ability to enter her brain whenever he wished, and if he somehow possessed the ability to push suggestions into the brains of unsuspecting people, forcing them to do horrible, sickening things, then what chance did she have to survive?

How could she protect herself against that kind of omnipresent threat? And what about everyone else in the world? Was Caitlyn Connelly going to become the vehicle, unwitting and unwilling as she may be, through which the notorious serial killer Milo Cain continued his reign of terror?

How could she live with herself if that was the case?

And did she even want to?

25

Virginia Ayers had never considered herself a particularly strong woman. She hadn't been able to prevent her husband from succumbing to deep depression and eventually committing suicide after their twins were born and then immediately given up in an illegal adoption.

Worse, she hadn't even seen it coming.

She hadn't been able to withstand the pain of Milo Cain's torture last summer, eventually giving in to his demands and calling Caitlyn and Kevin back to her home after she had sent them away to safety. That fateful telephone call had set all of this madness in motion, and although Virginia cherished every moment she had been able to spend with her daughter because of it, she would never forgive herself for subjecting Caitlyn to her unhinged twin's madness.

But for all her weakness, Virginia had always possessed the ability to do what was necessary. It was this personality trait that had allowed her to soldier on after giving up the twins for adoption the very same day they were born.

It was this personality trait that had allowed her to soldier on after Robert was found hanging in a men's bathroom at South Station so many years ago.

She was a survivor. She was someone who could do what had to be done. It wasn't much to brag about, not much to show for nearly six decades of life on this earth. But it was all she had.

And now she knew what had to be done. Sitting in the back of a cab as it raced across Boston toward Logan International Airport, staring into the terrified eyes of her only daughter, Virginia knew.

Caitlyn would never have a moment's peace the way things currently stood. She would never be able to let her guard down, would never feel safe. And the worst part was that her vigilance wouldn't even matter. At some point, whether on his next attempt or the one after that or the one after that, Milo would succeed in his quest to destroy his twin, the one who had been blessed with goodness and kindness and all of those traits so sorely lacking in himself.

He would succeed and Caitlyn would be gone, and Virginia would once again have lost both her children, three decades after the first time and this time for good.

As the cab pulled to a stop at Logan Airport's Terminal B, where they were scheduled to fly back to Tampa on board a National Airlines Boeing 757, Virginia made her decision. She would do what had to be done.

She held her daughter's right hand in both of hers, squeezing it gently. She ignored the impatient cabbie, who was waiting for them to climb out of the backseat so he could remove their luggage from the trunk and move on to his next fare.

She stared into Caitlyn's eyes and said, "You need to calm down. I can feel your fear. It's coming off you in waves."

Caitlyn shook her head. "It's hopeless. There's nothing I can do."

"You can get on this airplane and go home, for starters. Get a good night's sleep and I guarantee things will look better tomorrow."

"How is anything going to get better? And what do you mean, 'I' have to get on the airplane? Don't you mean, 'we'?"

"I didn't want to tell you until the last minute because I thought it would upset you," Virginia lied. "I talked to one of my old friends in Revere this morning on the phone and made plans. I'm going to spend tonight with her and then fly back to Tampa tomorrow."

Cait furrowed her brow. "When would you have had time to do that?"

The cabbie cleared his throat and grunted something in Bostonian. The words were unclear but the message was obvious: *Get out of my cab.*

"I did it while you were sleeping this morning, and with everything going on, I never got around to telling you until now. But don't worry, I'll be back in Tampa by tomorrow."

"I'll stay here with you."

"No, honey, you've never met my friend, and it will just be two old ladies making up stories about the good old days. Besides," she said. "I know how badly you want to get back to Tampa so you can be at Kevin's bail hearing." The hearing had been scheduled for 4:30 tomorrow, and Cait had told Virginia she was determined to make it back in time.

"I-I suppose," Cait said. She was clearly confused and her expression said she didn't believe Virginia's story, but by now the cabbie had begun to raise his voice and was demanding they get out. "We're holdin' up traffic!" he said with a wave of his meaty arm at the cars behind them.

And he was right. The line of cars at the terminal's sidewalk passenger drop-off had expanded quickly and now snaked out onto the access road. Soon the police would be along to unsnarl everything and get the traffic moving again.

Cait stepped reluctantly out of the car and Virginia followed behind her. As the driver pulled their suitcases out of the trunk she touched his arm and said, "Only my daughter will be flying out today. I need a ride to Revere, can you do that?"

The scowl on his face conveyed his impatience with her, but he nodded. He was clearly unhappy picking up a ten-minute fare at the airport—Revere was that close to East Boston—but Virginia knew he would change his tune once they were safely away from Cait and she could tell him the real destination.

Cait pointed out her suitcase and the driver lifted it out of the trunk and set it on the ground next to her. She lifted the handle and stepped up onto the sidewalk and Virginia hugged her tightly.

"I'll see you tomorrow," she said, knowing it was likely untrue. "And stay calm. Try not to worry. You'll get through this."

The driver interrupted. "I gotta go now. I can't afford to lose my airport medallion for you two. Get in if you want a ride."

He slid in behind the wheel and slammed his door. Virginia stepped back to the cab and got in as well.

And then they were gone. The last thing Virginia saw as they rounded the circular airport access road was her daughter still standing where she had been dropped off. She looked bewildered and afraid.

And utterly, completely alone.

26

Cait was now confused as well as terrified as she sat anxiously in the back of a cab. She doubted her mother had called anyone from their hotel room that morning, although she couldn't be one hundred percent certain. Virginia *had* been awake while she was sleeping. Cait recalled waking up to find her mother watching her from the other bed.

So she would have had the opportunity to make a call.

But wouldn't Cait have heard her talking? Cait's insomnia was so debilitating that she rarely slept more than a few minutes at a time, and even when she did, she slept extremely lightly. She didn't think there was any way Virginia could have had a telephone conversation from the same hotel room without awakening her, no matter how quietly she had spoken into her phone.

And who would she have called? Since moving to Tampa, Virginia rarely talked about her life back in Revere, and when she did, she never mentioned being close to any of her neighbors. In fact, just the opposite was true. She had confided in Cait many times that she practically became a shut-in after Robert's death. She rarely socialized and had no close friends.

So something was happening that Cait didn't understand. The plan all along had been for them to fly to Boston, get into Bridgewater State Hospital to convince themselves of Milo's helplessness, and then fly back to Tampa. Together.

Now her burgeoning fear—and it continued to build, despite her mother's reassurances—was joined by a profound confusion. If Virginia wasn't visiting an old friend tonight, and the more Cait thought about it the more she felt it was highly unlikely, then what in the world *was* she doing?

Cait took a deep breath and tried to put her fear and confusion aside, tried to focus on the excitement of seeing Kevin. He could be a free man, pending trial, in just a few hours. His bail hearing was scheduled to take place at 4:30 and despite his insistence she stay away, Cait was determined to be there if at all possible.

And it looked as though it would be possible.

Her taxi pulled to a stop in front of the George E. Edgecomb Courthouse, a modern-looking, seven-story office building with a circular entrance on Twiggs Street in downtown Tampa. The all-glass three-story entryway featured a large portico with columns in front and a sign announcing Thirteenth Judicial Circuit Court of Florida in silver banner lettering running along the top of the portico.

Cait paid the driver and hurried inside. Security was tight, typical of all modern courthouses, and she knew bringing a full suitcase into the building would be a problem. She might be denied entry with it, and even if she could convince the courthouse security force to hold the bag for her, the amount of time it would take to convince them to do so would probably result in her missing the hearing.

So she dropped it in a trash barrel and walked inside. She considered leaving it at the entrance in the hopes it would still be there when she came out, but knew that possibility was practically nil. And leaving a suspicious bag at the entrance to a municipal building like the Edgecomb Courthouse was a good way to get the entire place locked down for hours and possibly herself arrested as well.

She wouldn't miss the bag. Its contents were nothing more than a couple of cheap outfits and some toiletries, nothing she couldn't easily replace, and being present for Kevin's bail hearing was much more important to her than a couple of pairs of slacks and a blouse or two.

Inside, Cait waited for her turn to pass through the metal detector, checking her watch impatiently. There were only three people ahead of her but time was running out. It was going to be close. Moments later, she had emptied her pockets into a small basket, passed successfully through the metal detector, and recovered her belongings. Then she received directions to the criminal courtroom where Kevin's hearing would take place and hurried away.

Inside the courtroom, the gallery was half-filled. Some of the viewers were undoubtedly media members here to report on the case of the Tampa police officer who had attacked his live-in girlfriend with a carving knife. It was a juicy story, and Cait knew it would be followed closely until some other, juicier story took its place in the limelight. She hoped that would happen soon.

She slipped inside and took a seat in the back row. She wanted badly to see Kevin but didn't want to upset him after he had expressly instructed her to stay away. Glancing around the gallery, she saw no one she recognized. Cait didn't know all of Kevin's cop buddies, probably didn't even know most of them. But of the ones she knew, none had chosen to be here to support their friend and fellow officer.

After a few long minutes, as Cait's tension and fear—she was beginning to wonder if the fear would ever go away—steadily increased, a side door opened and Kevin entered the courtroom. He was dressed in an orange jailhouse jumpsuit, hands cuffed in front of him, accompanied by an armed bailiff.

The sight broke Cait's heart. Kevin was the finest, most upstanding man she had ever met and she knew this ordeal must be killing him. He appeared composed, however, and moved directly to the defendant's table, face impassive. He turned his back to her and took a seat next to his attorney. He never saw her.

27

Milo raged at the unmitigated gall of The Evil Bitch and Mommy Dearest. After they waltzed out of his room, he entertained himself with elaborate fantasies of the suffering he would visit upon them. Connelly would be first, and then the worthless vessel who had spawned her thirty years ago would get a turn.

He spent what felt like hours on this pleasurable exercise, and by the time he lost interest, Milo realized he was once again exhausted. Apparently one recovery cycle was not enough after leaping into some-one else's head. He drifted away and lost consciousness.

ONCE AGAIN, MILO HAD no way of knowing how long he had been unconscious when he woke up. But in any event, this time when he awakened, he felt refreshed and ready to go.

He felt like his old self again.

And that was fortunate, because there was a lot to do. He needed to come up with yet another plan of attack that would finally rid the world of Caitlyn Connelly. Once and for all. Her string of lucky escapes had led Milo to the inescapable conclusion that he had been too half-assed in his approach, had taken too much for granted.

That would now change. He resolved to take his time planning and to develop a strategy that would leave nothing to chance. His next at-tack would be his final attack.

First things first, though. He needed to learn exactly where The Evil Bitch and her mother were right now, and what they might be up to. Their little sortie inside Bridgewater State Hospital had unsettled Milo more than he would like to admit, because no matter how highly evolved he might be, how intellectually advanced, his physical body was his Achilles heel. He was as helpless as helpless could get.

Until he could finalize his plans for dealing with the only person in the world who posed any kind of real threat to him, Milo knew he would have to monitor her—and by extension, her mother—closely.

There was no alternative. It was time to get back inside Connelly's head.

HE WAS SURPRISED TO discover that she was inside a courtroom somewhere.

Interesting.

He absorbed the atmosphere with an interest bordering on fascination as Connelly took in her surroundings. Despite the fact Milo Cain was one of Massachusetts' most notorious serial killers, he had never entered a courthouse, had never stood trial for anything, had never spent a single day in jail.

His intelligence and cunning had managed to keep him several steps ahead of law enforcement his entire life. Until, of course, he ran into The Evil Bitch and her mother's goddamn handgun last summer.

His luck had run out at the most inopportune moment.

Milo felt the familiar agitation beginning to set in, the fury that seemed to overtake him whenever he even thought about his twin sister, and he forced himself to relax. This was a reconnaissance mission, nothing more, and for it to be effective, he had to set aside his animosity and gather information.

The first order of business was to determine why the hell The Evil Bitch might be sitting inside a courtroom. His assumption had been that she and Mommy Dearest had flown to Massachusetts for the sole purpose of gloating at him, of invading his territory to demonstrate their superiority. And they had done exactly that, to his impotent fury.

Why then would they have gone to court? What business could they possibly have in a Massachusetts courtroom?

Then a side door opened and Milo watched through Connelly's eyes as her boyfriend Kevin Dalton, the wannabe-hero cop from their little encounter last summer, was led into the courtroom in handcuffs.

Thunderstruck, Milo realized Caitlyn Connelly was no longer *in* Massachusetts. She had accomplished her goal of humiliating Milo and had apparently flown right back to Florida to support the man who had tried to slice her open.

This must be a bail hearing.

Milo smiled inside his head. He couldn't believe his incredible luck. This was too good to be true. A large part of Milo Cain's genius, and the main reason he had been able to elude authorities for over a decade despite committing atrocities of the sort rarely seen outside the bloodiest horror movies, was his ability to adjust to changing circumstances.

When he had been active as "Mr. Midnight," haunting the streets of Boston in search of victims to torture in his own unique way, Milo had possessed almost a supernatural sixth sense regarding the authorities' search for the elusive serial killer. While the cops concentrated their efforts on protecting the city's large population of college girls, Milo would carve up a few hookers.

Eventually the dolts would change their strategy and focus their efforts on protecting the prostitute population. Every time they did, with unerring instincts, at exactly the right moment Milo would adjust his priorities, targeting the college girls the police had previously been so keen on protecting and who were now ripe for the picking.

Those instincts hadn't abandoned him over the past six months, regardless of his bad luck back in Revere last summer, and they were screaming at him that this was a clear opportunity. This was an unexpected chance to fuck with The Evil Bitch in a way that would be just as satisfying as a direct attack on her physically.

If nothing else, it would buy him time until he developed a plan to finish her off for good.

He took in the proceedings, biding his time, watching Kevin Dalton carefully through Connelly's eyes. It was simple, much easier than it had been last night at The Crow's Nest. Today, she practically stared a hole through her precious boyfriend as he sat quietly at the defense table.

Milo realized his assumption had been correct. Kevin Dalton was in court today for a bail hearing. And to listen to the defense tell it, there was no reason in the world why this man should not be allowed to walk free pending trial. He was a solid citizen, so the argument went. A police officer, charged with protecting the citizens of Tampa, and possessed an exemplary work record.

He'd performed his duties as a law enforcement officer to a consistently high standard. He'd never been in trouble with the law prior to last Friday night. There was no reason to consider him a flight risk.

Even the prosecution team, although attempting to summon the standard prosecutorial indignation at the notion that anyone charged with a crime might be permitted bail, didn't seem to have their hearts in it. It was apparent to Milo that they recognized the futility of their position and appeared content to surrender this round basically uncontested.

Milo intended to change all that.

THE MOMENT THE NOW-familiar pressure started building inside her skull, Cait knew bad things were about to happen. Whether as a result of some strange ability by Milo Cain or something else entirely, the cause and effect of this phenomenon had by now become as clear as day: cranial pressure equaled some unfortunate and likely painful outcome.

The onset of the pressure was once again accompanied by sharp pain. Each time the phenomenon had occurred, the pain had gotten steadily more severe, and today was no exception. It shot through her brain like the crack of a whip, and Cait clutched her temples and gasped, lowering her head and closing her eyes, praying the intense discomfort would recede within seconds as it had in the past.

The courtroom observers closest to her furrowed their eyebrows and glanced in her direction, either out of concern for her wellbeing or annoyance at the interruption. One middle-aged woman seated in front of her leaned back and asked quietly, "Are you all right, dear?"

Five seconds dragged into ten, during which time the pain inside her skull was so intense Cait could do no more than concentrate on staying conscious, of trying not to collapse to the floor. This was by far the worst occurrence yet.

Then the vise that had been tightening on her brain loosened and the discomfort began to melt away. The amount of time she had spent caught in the grip of the pain was no longer than any of the previous instances, but the intensity of that pain was far worse this time than it had ever been.

Cait wondered fleetingly about the damage being done to her brain by...whatever was happening. But this wasn't the time to worry about that. Now that the sheer agony had receded, she had other, much more immediate concerns.

She realized the woman two rows in front was still waiting for an answer. She lifted her head and whispered, "Yes, I'm fine, thank you."

She didn't bother to express her terror. What would she say? *I'm actually not fine. I'm about as far from fine as I could possibly be. I'm not even within shouting distance of fine. If you want to know the truth, I'm terrified that my comatose, paralyzed twin, who happens to be an in-*

famous serial killer, is about to wreak havoc in this courtroom and I'm afraid, really and truly afraid, that I might be about to die.

But she said nothing. Instead, she offered a trembling smile to the older woman, who gave her an odd look and then turned back around, focusing her attention once more on the front of the courtroom. The judge didn't seem to have noticed the minor spectacle, nor had the prosecution or defense teams.

Cait worked to control her breathing, not wanting to hyperventilate and pass out right here in the courthouse. If this sensation inside her head meant Milo was somehow here, sharing space in her brain, she didn't know what horrible things he might be able to accomplish if she lost consciousness, or what devastation she might awaken to find.

Or whether she would ever awaken at all.

She lowered her head for a moment and closed her eyes. *Get a grip, dammit.* Then she opened them and tried to convince herself she was prepared for anything. It didn't work.

She looked around the courtroom suspiciously. Nothing seemed out of place. Everyone looked perfectly normal, or as normal as was possible for a bail hearing in criminal court.

Returning her attention to Kevin, Cait tamped down her fear and tried to concentrate. She was here to support him and was damned well going to do exactly that. She would focus on him while remaining alert to the possibility—or rather, the likelihood—of impending violence.

The hearing moved quickly, the defense making every effort to secure Kevin's release, the prosecution not seeming too terribly committed to preventing it. Cait began to rally, feeling a little optimism beginning to compete with her fear. She was no trial lawyer, hadn't stepped foot inside a courtroom prior to today since graduating law school. But it looked good for Kevin.

He was sitting ramrod-straight behind the defense table, flanked by a pair of attorneys, and as Cait watched, his head twitched noticeably.

The movement was unnatural, as if he'd been slapped across the face by an invisible hand.

Instantly her cautious optimism turned to horror. His actions so resembled those of Friday night, just before he attacked her in their apartment, that Cait felt as though she could have been watching an instant replay. His back was to her, but if she had been able to get a good look into his eyes, she knew exactly what she would see: a blank, glassy stare.

Her worst fears were being confirmed.

For a second or two following his odd head-shake, Kevin sat perfectly still. The prosecuting attorney was busy addressing the judge, questioning some minor point advanced by the defense team.

All eyes were on that attorney.

Except for Cait's.

She watched in horror as Kevin lifted his hands—still manacled together at the wrists—onto the table. No one else noticed him pick up a pen that had been lying on top of a yellow legal pad and clutch it in his right fist.

In one smooth motion, Kevin rose to his feet and turned to face the defense attorney sitting to his left. Cait screamed a half second before Kevin lifted the pen to shoulder height and then slashed downward.

The lawyer reacted late, caught off-guard. He tried to propel himself backward, over his chair and onto the floor, exactly as Cait had done last night at The Crow's Nest, but he was too slow. The pen caught the lawyer in the neck and opened a jagged gash. Blood spurted, crimson and thick, splattering onto the lawyer and Kevin as chaos erupted in the courtroom. People screamed and some of the gallery members closest to the defense table began pushing and shoving in a desperate attempt to escape the danger.

Cait continued to scream as the bailiff fumbled for the gun in his holster, finally bringing it to bear on Kevin just as he lifted his hands and advanced on the stricken lawyer. Both of the victim's hands were clamped against his neck in an effort to stanch the flow of blood, which continued leaking heavily around his fingers.

The bailiff hesitated. If he fired and the bullet missed Kevin, he would likely strike someone in the gallery. He began shuffling forward across the courtroom, gun trained on Kevin, screaming something that was lost in the din.

Kevin took a step toward the lawyer, who was scrabbling sideways across the floor in the general direction of the prosecutor's table. Kevin stepped in a slick pool of blood and then lost his footing, spilling to the floor almost on top of the terrified attorney.

The bailiff saw his opportunity. He still couldn't risk a shot, but the moment Kevin dropped in a heap, the man leaped forward. He skidded to a stop in the blood next to Kevin and the injured lawyer. Leaned down. Placed the barrel of his weapon against the side of Kevin's head.

The initial frenzy of screaming had abated, as onlookers realized they weren't being targeted. Yet.

The bailiff shouted, "Freeze and drop the weapon or you die!"

Kevin ignored the warning. It was almost as if the man hadn't even spoken. He squirmed up onto his knees to take another stab at his attorney, and the bailiff reared back and smashed the butt of his gun into the side of Kevin's skull.

Kevin wobbled but stayed on his knees.

The bailiff pistol-whipped him again, and this time Kevin toppled onto his side and lay still, the blood of his victim soaking into his jailhouse jumpsuit.

Cait had stopped screaming but could feel tears running down her cheeks. She was crying heavily but hadn't even realized it until now. She stared in horror, unable to turn her gaze away from her unconscious lover even for a second, and she felt the pressure inside her head disappear just as abruptly as it had come.

For a long moment no one moved and the courtroom was eerily silent. Then police backup arrived and chaos erupted again.

28

C ait sat at her kitchen table staring out the window, seeing nothing. The Tampa skyline twinkled, plenty of lights still shining despite the lateness of the hour. In the distance, the Gulf of Mexico lay vast and dark and empty.

She glanced at the clock on the wall and then back out the window. She realized she hadn't noticed the time, but didn't care. A cup of tea in front of her sat untouched. It had long since cooled to an undrinkable temperature.

It had taken hours to get home after the awful events inside the Edgecomb Courthouse. Police in riot gear had stormed in and hustled Kevin away, his arms locked tightly behind his back, his eyes blank and unseeing.

He wasn't himself. Literally.

After securing the scene, the police had taken statements from all the witnesses, including Cait. She related everything she saw, leaving out nothing but her certainty that for the second time in less than four days, Kevin's actions had been not his own but those of Milo Cain.

There was no reason to tell them that part. The authorities would have rejected Cait's theory outright, and she couldn't blame them. Nothing in their experience—hell, nothing in *anyone's* experience—would have given them reason to believe her. There certainly wasn't any physical evidence to support her position, nothing that could be collected and analyzed under a microscope, no data that could be placed in an evidence locker and used in a trial.

Nothing.

So Cait had kept her fears, or more accurately her certainties, about Milo Cain to herself. Everything else she told the investigators. Her voice never wavered; the tears never returned.

As she spoke, she felt as empty as Kevin had looked. It would take the most extreme self-delusion to think Kevin would have a chance at being released on bail now, and Cait realized that was for the best. Milo was using Kevin as a blunt instrument to torture her. If he couldn't attack her directly, he would attack innocent bystanders like the poor defense attorney, who had nearly been killed in the brutal, unprovoked assault.

After giving her statement, Cait had been told she was free to go. She left the courthouse to the glare of television lights and the shouted questions of reporters, who were clustered behind yellow police crime-scene tape but who screamed their questions anyway, undeterred.

She ignored them.

Hailed a cab.

Rode home in silence.

And had been sitting in her kitchen ever since, thinking.

It was over. Milo had won. He lay in a prison hospital bed, injured, as helpless as a newborn baby. And yet somehow he could still terrorize innocent people in the most horrific of ways. He would always be able to terrorize innocent people. Somehow her twin brother, the cold, unfeeling sociopath who had tortured and murdered young women—the exact number of his victims was still unknown and probably always would be—in a decade-long killing spree, had managed to cheat death, and in doing so had liberated himself from his broken body.

And he would never give up until he destroyed her.

For the first time in her life, Cait felt utterly defeated. She could not win and she could not escape. Milo would kill her, if not today, then tomorrow. If not tomorrow, then next week or next month or next year. The best she could hope for was that no other innocents would suffer the way the injured defense attorney had suffered tonight. The way Kevin was suffering right now.

She thought about suicide, considered the topic in a way she never had before, running the notion around in her head not as a theoretical concept, but as a concrete possibility. Could she do it? Would she be able to take her own life?

Her father had done so. He had been so consumed with guilt and regret he had hung himself in a public place.

So it was in her genes.

But suppose she did kill herself. Suppose she surrendered to Milo's vicious campaign against her. Suppose she stepped off a chair with a noose snugged around her neck, or ingested a full bottle of prescription medication, or borrowed her mother's pistol and fired a bullet into her brain.

Suppose she did it.

Suppose.

What would happen then? Would Milo quit? Would he miraculously see the error of his ways and give up the commission of torture? Would he remove himself from the human race and waste away inside his paralyzed body back at Bridgewater State Hospital?

Of course he would not. He would never change; he *could* never change. Milo Cain was as incapable of growing a conscience as Caitlyn Connelly was of picking up a knife and attacking an innocent person.

So suicide would accomplish nothing. In fact, Cait now realized, killing herself would only make the situation worse.

At least now, while Milo was obsessed with torturing Cait, his attention was more or less diverted from the rest of the population. Yes, he had used Kevin to attack an innocent bystander, but his message was clear, at least to Cait. He was out to get her. The attorney was nothing more than collateral damage.

And once he completed his deadly business with her, he would be free to turn his vicious psychopathy on truly innocent people. All the time. As much as he wanted, whenever he wanted.

Rather than making Cait feel better, this realization only deepened her sense of hopelessness. There was nothing she could do to help herself *or* anyone else.

She looked up at the kitchen clock again and then away.

But what difference did the time make?

What difference did anything make?

Cait continued staring out the window, unseeing.

29

Virginia managed to rent the same hotel room she had stayed in with Caitlyn the previous night. Her first thought after leaving her daughter at the airport had been to go straight back to Bridgewater and request another visit with Milo.

With Caitlyn out of earshot, she had gone as far as giving the change of destination to the cabdriver, who had been thrilled with the prospect of another thirty-five-mile fare, especially after she had told him initially that she only needed to get to Revere.

But the man's mood took a sharp turn for the worse when she changed her mind again. The Squire Hotel was an even shorter trip than anywhere in Revere would have been, and his scowl at hearing this latest development would have terrified the average traveler.

Not Virginia Ayers. After all she had been through in her life she was by now nothing like the average traveler. She barely noticed the driver's annoyance and certainly didn't care. She had seen much more frightening things than an angry cabbie.

When the sullen man pulled to a stop in front of the hotel, yanking the wheel to the right and slamming on the brakes like a NASCAR driver pulling into pit row, Virginia smiled and thanked him for his patience. He didn't even respond. But when she paid the fare and then gave the man a hundred-dollar tip, his demeanor changed one last time. His eyes widened and he smiled brightly and then he pulled away from the curb in a squeal of burning rubber, serenaded by a chorus of honking horns.

THE LAST THING VIRGINIA wanted to do was spend another day in Boston. But she knew if she didn't handle the Milo situation properly, she might not be allowed into Bridgewater State Hospital again, not just today but maybe not ever.

She and Caitlyn had been given a special time slot, outside of normal prison visiting hours, to see Milo today, and Virginia was savvy enough to know that alienating the warden by ignoring the previously established protocol on a second visit—unannounced, no less—would accomplish nothing good.

So she booked herself back into the Squire. She would use the time to follow all the rules to the letter, coordinating another visit with Milo tomorrow. Then she could get back where she belonged, by Caitlyn's side.

"BRIDGEWATER STATE HOSPITAL, Nancy Bickford speaking, how may I help you?" The voice on the other end of the telephone line was cool and professional, a far cry from the Nancy Bickford who had become so emotional recalling the death of her former boss earlier in the day.

"Hello, Nancy, my name is Virginia Ayers. I was at the facility this morning today with my daughter. We were there to visit Milo Cain."

"Of course," the warden's secretary said. "I trust your visit went well?"

"Yes it did, thank you for asking. I'm hoping to coordinate a second visit tomorrow, at the same time if possible."

"A second visit?" The woman's confusion was evident. Virginia couldn't blame her for not understanding. How much could there be to say to a patient/inmate who was no more animated than a lump of coal?

"That's right. I'm calling because I know Warden Ciuffetti was reluctant to approve visitors for Milo during normal visiting hours and I assume her preference would be the same for tomorrow."

There was a long silence as Nancy Bickford considered the request. "I don't know..." she said. "This will have to go through the warden and I'm not sure she's available."

"Would you mind checking?" Virginia said. "I would be the only visitor this time. My daughter's already gone back to Florida and I'm hoping to be able to fly out tomorrow afternoon, but before I do, I would really like to see my son one more time. I'm not sure when—or even if—I'll get another opportunity. You see, I've been ill for quite some time, and I may not be well enough to return to the area again."

Another silence. Then, "I'll see if she's in."

After a delay of at least five minutes, during which time Virginia spent wondering what the hell she would do if her request was denied, Warden Ciuffetti came on the line. "Hello, Mrs. Ayers. I understand you'd like to make arrangements to see Inmate Cain again tomorrow."

"That's right. If it's not too much trouble." Virginia repeated the song and dance about seeing her son one last time, knowing all the while exactly what the other woman was thinking: *why didn't you say your good-byes when you were here a few hours ago?*

It was a logical question; one for which Virginia had no good answer. She prayed Warden Ciuffetti wouldn't ask it and was relieved when she didn't. After some more back and forth and what felt like an inordinately long amount of time and energy wasted on what was a simple request, the warden issued her approval, offering an appointment at the same time as today's.

"That would be wonderful," Virginia said sincerely. "Thank you for your consideration."

"Not a problem," Warden Ciuffetti answered, although it had certainly *seemed* like a problem. "When you get here tomorrow, simply check in at the front desk and you'll be escorted to Inmate Cain's room. There will be no need to stop at my office again."

"Outstanding," Virginia said. "Thank you so much."

30

It was not yet seven a.m. when Virginia's cell phone rang. She was awake, but hadn't showered or begun getting ready for the day. The phone's caller ID function showed that the number was Cait's.

A call this early could not be good.

"Hello?" Virginia hated to lie to Cait as she had done yesterday at the airport, but was prepared to double down if necessary with a further story about staying with a neighbor friend should Cait revisit the subject of Virginia staying in Boston an extra day.

She didn't have to. Cait's voice was hushed. Hollow. Defeated. "It's never going to end," she said.

Something was obviously very wrong. "What happened?" Virginia said.

"It's Milo. It has to be Milo."

"What about Milo?"

"He's done it again."

"Caitlyn, honey, you have to explain what's going on."

"You know how I wanted to get back here so I could be at Kevin's bail hearing?"

The dull throb of a headache began at the base of Virginia's skull. "Yes, I know. What happened?"

"It has to be Milo. I've been thinking about it all night and there's no other explanation. It's Milo, and he's never going to stop, and there's no way to *make* him stop."

"Caitlyn, please, back up and tell me everything."

So she did.

By the time Cait was done talking, Virginia began to fear she might not be able to make it to Bridgewater in time for her appointment. She didn't want to hurry her daughter along, though, because she had never heard Cait's voice this dead. This devoid of hope.

"Kevin is a strong young man," she said. "He'll get through this and so will you."

The silence on the other end of the line reminded Virginia of last night while she was waiting to talk to Warden Ciuffetti. But this was much worse. Instead of impatience at the lack of a response, she felt a very real fear for her child. It sounded like Cait had given up.

She decided to try a different tack. "Listen to me," she said. "We don't even know for certain that Milo is responsible for what's going on—"

"It's him," Cait said vehemently. "I'm certain of it, even if you're not." It was the first spark of life she'd shown in the conversation.

"Okay, even if it is him, things have a way of changing, often when you least expect them to."

"How are they going to change? There's no way to stop him. It's impossible."

"Just take things one step at a time, honey. Can you do that for me?"

"It's the only thing I *can* do. I'm completely at a loss for ideas."

"Are you at home?"

"Yes."

"Good. Why don't you stay there until you hear from me again? I'll be leaving for Tampa in a little while and I'll need a ride home from the airport when I arrive. Do you think you could pick me up?"

Cait paused and then said, "Of course."

"Caitlyn, you sound awful. How much sleep did you get last night?"

"I didn't."

"You didn't sleep at all?"

"No. How could I?"

Virginia ran a hand tiredly over her face. She had just gotten up and she was already exhausted. And it was going to be a very long day. "Okay, Cait, listen to me. Try to get some rest and I'll call you as soon as I know what time my flight will be landing this afternoon."

They disconnected the call and Virginia sighed deeply. She wondered whether there was any reason to believe the reassurance she had tried to give her daughter. It was clear Cait didn't.

She wasn't sure she did, either.

IT WAS FIVE MINUTES after ten when she walked through the metal detector at Bridgewater State Hospital. The guard manning the front entrance remembered her from yesterday and gave her a smile. "Back again so soon?" he said.

Virginia forced herself to return his smile, although it was the last thing she felt like doing. She was nervous and afraid and thought she had a pretty good idea how a prisoner walking to the electric chair might feel.

"I don't know when I'll have the chance to return," she said, "so I wanted to pay Milo one last visit while I still can."

"Flying solo today?"

"Excuse me?"

"Where's your daughter?"

"Oh, she's back in Florida. Yes, it's just me this time."

Virginia had emptied her pockets and now she stepped through the metal detector. She gathered up her things as the guard pressed a button on a console and spoke into a telephone handset.

A moment later, another guard appeared through a doorway and signaled for Virginia to follow. It was a different door than the one she and Cait had gone through yesterday to get to the warden's office, and she assumed this corridor would lead directly to the medical wing and Milo's room.

She didn't recognize this guard. He was polite and respectful and made innocuous small talk as they navigated through the complex. Virginia tried to engage him as best she could, but the deeper they descended into the bowels of the ancient structure, the blacker her mood seemed to get.

After what felt like an eternity—the route must have been a shortcut compared to yesterday's trip from the warden's office to the hospital ward, but it sure didn't feel like it—they rounded a corner and approached Milo's room from the opposite direction.

At the door, the guard turned the handle and waved Virginia inside. She thanked him and walked into the room and was horrified when the man entered behind her.

This was unacceptable. She needed to be alone for her plan to have any chance at all of succeeding. Even then it was probably a fool's errand. But with an armed prison guard standing less than five feet away, she had no chance.

She should have known better than to think this guard would ignore the rules as yesterday's had. Undoubtedly it was against regulations for any visitor to be left alone with a prisoner. The fact that this particular prisoner was totally immobile, helpless and unable to attempt escape under any circumstances must have convinced yesterday's guard to give Virginia and Cait a little privacy.

Virginia now realized she had been stupid not to plan for this. The fear and desperation she had been experiencing all morning ratcheted up even further, and she struggled to keep from fleeing the room, from rushing past the guard and running for the exit.

Instead she stood motionless, conscious of the guard's presence behind her and of her son's still form in front of her. She had to do something, so she turned and looked up at the guard and told him the truth.

"I've come to say good-bye to my son," she said. "This is the last time I'll ever see him, I'm far too ill to do this again and it's far too painful. May I please have a few minutes alone with him?"

The guard hesitated, clearly weighing regulations against his humane desire to allow an anguished mother a little time to try to achieve some sort of peace. She thought he was going to refuse her, but after a moment he said, "Of course. I'll be right outside if you need me."

And just like that, Virginia was alone with Milo. She inched forward and stood next to his hospital bed. Like yesterday, his right wrist was handcuffed to the stainless steel bed rail. She looked down at him, filled with fear and regret and a longing for things that had never been and things that could never be.

He was a monster, she knew that. Virginia Ayers had lived too long and undergone too much heartache to fool herself into believing anything else. She wouldn't have been able to even if she tried.

Milo Cain was irreparably broken and had been his entire life. His paralysis and coma were not symptoms of his illness but rather the result of it. The world would be better off with Milo out of it. She was as certain of that as she had been of anything in her life.

But he was still her son. Her flesh and blood. Milo's body was pale, wasted, muscles mostly atrophied after more than six months of total paralysis. Nevertheless, as she stood next to his bed gazing into his slack features, the resemblance to her long-dead husband was clear. She looked into his face and saw Robert, and the tears welled up in her eyes, tears she had not shed in many years. Tears she had long ago thought herself incapable of shedding anymore.

But this was not Robert, and the resemblance of the son to the father changed nothing about what she had come here to do. What she *must* do if she was to have any chance of saving at least one member of her doomed family. She closed her eyes and gave thanks to a God she had long since stopped acknowledging, that Robert Ayers had not lived to see the atrocities committed by his only son.

Or the one she was here to commit.

She picked up Milo's hand and held it between both of hers. It was larger than hers, but not by much. It felt cool and bony, wasted away like the rest of his body until resembling nothing so much as a skeleton tightly covered by an almost translucent wrap, a wrap that looked like skin but felt brittle and delicate, like centuries-old parchment.

His skin felt almost alien, which struck Virginia as most appropriate. Milo Cain *was* an alien. Not in the commonly accepted sense of the word—he hadn't come down from the sky in a spacecraft from another world—but he might as well have. His bizarre abilities and shattered personality had made him as unlike the rest of humanity as any space alien could ever have been.

Virginia blinked herself back to reality and realized she had been standing here ruminating on her poor son's miserable fate for far too long. She didn't know how long the guard would wait outside in the hallway before checking on things inside the inmate's room.

She couldn't afford to waste what precious little time she had left.

She let go of Milo's hand. Turned and checked the door. It was still closed, and the tiny reinforced-glass window revealed nothing on the other side. No guard. No nurses or doctors scurrying along the hallway. Nothing.

Virginia Ayers turned back to her son and said softly, "I'm so sorry, Milo. I'm so sorry for everything."

She lifted his head with her left hand—it was much heavier than she had expected—and removed one of the two pillows it had been resting on.

Then she lowered his head gently to the remaining pillow.

With one last glance toward the still-empty hallway, Virginia Ayers grasped the pillow in both hands, one on either side, and dropped it onto her son's face. She pressed it firmly against his nose and mouth and eased down with a steady but relentless pressure.

There was no struggle.

No movement.

Nothing at all to indicate Virginia Ayers was suffocating her own child to death.

31

Milo was dozing when the door to his room opened. He snapped awake, confused as to the time and the purpose of the visit. Existing primarily in the spiritual realm—as was the case for him now—had its advantages, but being tethered to a weak and unresponsive body carried with it certain obvious risks, especially when you were one of the most hated and feared men in America.

So he listened closely. Was this a visit to change his linens? Change his colostomy bag? Bathe him?

The nurses who normally attended to his physical needs didn't waste their breath speaking to him—why would they?—but in most instances, they worked in pairs and their visits were marked by the constant inane chattering of young-adult women. Milo had spent many hours in blissful contemplation of what he would have done with their supple bodies were he not an inanimate mass of deteriorating flesh.

For a moment there was no noise at all, a situation that concerned Milo. It was simply not in the nurses' DNA to work quietly. Even on the rare occasions when only one young woman came in to attend to him, the nurse would invariably entertain herself by singing or humming under her breath, or talking to herself while texting on her phone, or doing something else to rein in her revulsion at having to care for Milo Cain, the notorious Mr. Midnight.

The swishing of clothing told him that someone was definitely inside the room. He was not imagining things. He waited, on edge, for something to happen.

And then Virginia Ayers spoke.

It was the last voice in the world he expected to hear. After popping into The Evil Bitch Connelly's head and discovering she was back in Florida, Milo had made the obvious and reasonable assumption that Mommy Dearest had flown south as well.

Clearly that was not the case.

Milo was so surprised at this development that he almost missed what the old biddy said. And it was significant: "I've come to say good-bye to my son. This is the last time I'll ever see him, I'm far too ill to do this again and it's far too painful. May I please have a few minutes alone with him?"

The guards had become lackadaisical regarding security procedures, at least where Milo was concerned, not that he blamed them. He was the subject of a monthly examination by the prison doctor, and the quack had consistently made the same diagnosis: there was simply no evidence to suggest Milo would ever come out of his coma. And even if by some miracle he did, he would remain paralyzed from the neck down. Forever.

Thus there was little reason for the guards to be concerned about the pathetic excuse for a human being wasting away in his hospital bed, his right wrist chained to the bed rail. It therefore came as no surprise when the guard agreed to wait outside. Milo strained to hear his voice, to determine which of the many Bridgewater State Prison guards had accompanied his mother on her visit, but he was disappointed as the man spoke softly, almost inaudibly, before disappearing through the door and then closing it behind him.

No matter. Milo was intrigued but not worried. Virginia Ayers had seemingly been on her last legs six months ago, weak and old beyond her years. And when Milo had been inside The Evil Bitch's head at The Crow's Nest, he had been surprised—though gladdened—when Connelly looked at their mother. The last few months had definitely not been kind to her, and she had gone even further downhill physically.

So there was no threat here. Virginia was undoubtedly going to pour her heart out over her son's comatose body, secure in the knowledge he could hear none of her twaddle. She would cry and wail in self-recrimination, stroking his brow with her ancient veiny hand as she tried to determine where she had gone so wrong.

It would be a few minutes of entertainment, a welcome break from the endless boredom of his day.

But nothing happened. Milo heard the rustle of clothing again as his mother approached his bed and then stopped. The flood of words he anticipated did not materialize. If she was crying, she was doing it quietly.

After a time, he sensed she picked up his hand and held it in hers. He couldn't feel it, of course, as he could feel nothing in his body below the neck. But still he knew it. He just did. And he was repulsed. It was awful enough to realize he was related by blood to this dried-up old witch, but to actually be touched by her? To be violated by the touch of her cadaverous hands on his skin?

It was torture of the vilest order. It made the things he had done to all of the young women over the last ten years seem like child's play. *This* was truly inhuman.

And there was nothing he could do about it. He had no control over his muscles, could not escape Virginia Ayers's clutches no matter how badly he might want to. He waited for it to be over, waited for her to feel she had accomplished whatever silly goal she had set for herself here, so she would turn around and leave forever.

The minutes seemed to stretch into eternity. Milo's sense of the passage of time had badly deteriorated after being comatose for six months, but still it seemed as though something should be happening. Anything.

At last the old hag spoke, so softly he could barely hear her words, even though she was standing right next to him. "I'm so sorry, Milo. I'm so sorry for everything."

This was not what he had expected. The words, yes, but not the tone accompanying them. She didn't sound hopeless and despairing; she sounded regretful but determined.

Like she had reached a decision that she hated to have to make, but had come to realize she was strong enough to carry it through. Alarm bells began going off in Milo Cain's head, the same alarm bells that had allowed him to stay ahead of the authorities for a decade as he had carried out his reign of terror in Boston.

Something was wrong.

Something was more than wrong.

Almost before he realized what was happening, Milo felt pressure on his face, on the one part of his broken body that could still experience the sensation of touch.

It was so unusual, it had been so long since he had experienced any physical feeling of any kind, that for a moment he could not quite process it.

Then the pressure increased dramatically, and Milo began to feel hazy and confused. Blackness began to envelop him, like a thick curtain had been dropped on his head and was choking out the light as it fluttered to the ground all around him.

She was killing him.

The ancient hag was killing him.

She had covered his nose and mouth with something, probably one of his pillows or a blanket, and was smothering the life out of him.

The blackness thickened. Milo came as close to surrendering to unthinking panic as he ever had. He was seconds from dropping into the abyss. The lights were flickering out. Quickly.

And he did the only thing he could think of in his weakened and desperate state.

He jumped into Virginia Ayers's head.

If he was going to die, maybe he could take the old bitch with him.

32

Virginia pressed more firmly on the pillow, using all the leverage she could muster out of her rail-thin body. She was shaking and breathing heavily, nearly hyperventilating from the stress. The guard might poke his head through the door at any moment to check on them and she needed to finish this awful task NOW.

The lack of struggle put up by Milo Cain's wasted body was the most horrifying part of this terrible chore. She should have expected it—he had been paralyzed for over six months, after all—but for some reason she hadn't considered her son's utter helplessness when she had concocted her plan.

The ease with which she could end another human being's life was shocking. It was worse than she could ever have imagined. And she wasn't strangling just any other person; she was killing her own flesh and blood. *Filicide*, she thought, *is the term for the murder of one's own child.*

It was a sterile, stark term for a messy and horrifying experience.

With Milo not struggling, Virginia wasn't sure when she should ease up on the pressure. The last thing she wanted was to allow air into Milo's lungs prematurely, to misjudge and find out later that he had somehow survived.

As appalling as was the notion of killing her own child, the only thing worse would be to allow him to live and continue tearing people's lives apart. His madness had destroyed enough innocent victims. The damage had to end now.

She found a reserve of strength and leaned even harder into the pillow. She would push for another thirty seconds and then—

—Virginia recoiled as if she had been slapped. Her brain felt...strange...like she was suffering from a severe head cold that had attacked her in an instant, rather than over the course of a couple of days.

It wasn't a headache.

It wasn't pain exactly, it was more like...

An ice-cold feeling of dread overtook Virginia Ayers as the significance of what had just happened struck her like a punch to the gut.

Pressure.

The feeling in her head was pressure.

Like what Caitlyn had been experiencing.

It was Milo.

Milo had insinuated himself into her skull even as she was snuffing the life out of him. He had left his own body and entered hers.

She hadn't considered the possibility that he might be able to do to her what he had been doing to Caitlyn all along. She *should* have considered it; both Caitlyn and Milo were her own flesh and blood, constructed from the same genetic makeup and cursed with the same awful family history.

Of course he would be able to jump into her head.

But it doesn't matter. He can't survive much longer. Once I've...finished...this horrible business, it will all be over.

She pushed even harder, her exhausted arms burning from the effort. Jammed the pillow into her paralyzed son's face, using one hand to apply pressure to the area of his nose and the other to apply it to his mouth.

She tried to guess how long he had been without air, but couldn't.

She continued her grim task, red-faced and sweating, panting from exertion, desperate for this nightmare to be over. For her grisly task to be complete.

At last she stopped, exhausted. Then she straightened. Lifted the pillow off her helpless child's face, the face of a monster.

He looked exactly the same as he had before she started. There was no bruising that she could detect, no blood, nothing to indicate he had been attacked as he lay defenseless in his bed.

Virginia glanced back at the door. It was still closed, and although she could barely see out the small, reinforced rectangular window from this angle, she knew no one was looking in at her, because if anyone *had* been watching, she would be in handcuffs right now.

She turned back toward Milo and leaned down over his face. Placed her ear as close to his mouth as she could manage, suddenly certain his eyes were going to spring open and he would snarl like a wild animal, like a wild animal that was ravenously hungry, and he would open his jaws wide, so wide that they would encompass his entire face, and his breath would be fetid, and rows and rows of jagged yellow shark's teeth would arise out of blackened gums, and he would close his jaws around her head, and he would—

No. I won't do this.

Milo Cain's body was irreparably shattered. He was comatose and paralyzed. He could no more use his jaws to rip her head off than he could jump out of bed and dance to a medley of show tunes.

But she had to know he was dead.

She had to know for sure.

Because her terror continued to build.

She placed her ear against her son's slack, half-open mouth. His lips were still warm, but that didn't mean anything. They wouldn't have had time to cool yet. She waited, getting her breathing a little more under control. Her heart continued to hammer in her chest like she had just run the Boston Marathon.

After thirty seconds she lifted her head. He wasn't breathing. There had been not the slightest wisp of an exhalation tickling her ear.

To be certain, she grasped his wrist, the one still shackled to the bed rail, in her trembling hands and felt lightly for a pulse.

Nothing.

Milo Cain was dead.

She had succeeded.

And she had failed.

Because the feeling of pressure inside her head was still there, and it was just as strong as it had been while murdering her only son.

33

Milo waited for the darkness to overtake him, for his brain to snap off, for consciousness to disappear like the devil had flipped a switch.

It didn't happen. He was alive.

And he was dead.

He watched through Virginia Ayers's eyes as she examined his prone form, double-checking her homicidal handiwork. She leaned down and felt/listened for evidence of continued breathing. She felt his wrist for a pulse.

Seeing his own body unmoving in the hospital bed was jarring. He hadn't been able to see himself since sometime before being shot last summer, and the way he looked now, pale and sickly, wasted, was in stark contrast to the way he remembered himself.

Not that he had ever been handsome. He had never been a big man; certainly had not been muscular or athletic.

But this...this pathetic creature lying dead in front of him/Virginia was something out of a bad horror movie. The figure was pale, with slack features and absolutely no muscle tone. It was one step above a skeleton, and the more Milo contemplated the shriveled body, the more he realized that particular comparison might reasonably be considered unfair to the skeleton.

But all of that was beside the point. He was still here. His body was dead but his consciousness lived on. Granted, he was—for the moment, at least—stuck inside the body of a frail geriatric murderess, but he had survived the worst sort of treachery imaginable, and would live (more or less) to fight another day.

How long he would be able to coexist inside this wretched excuse for a human being was debatable, but as long as he was able to think and to plan, he guessed he would be just fine.

In some ways, this situation was an improvement over his recent past. Now, instead of spending most of his time alone and lost inside the prison of his own useless body, he would be mobile, free to push thoughts and suggestions into unsuspecting passersby at will.

It was only a matter of time before the conniving, traitorous Virginia Ayers—Milo contemplated the murder she had just pulled off with a kind of paternalistic pride, not having believed Mommy Dearest capable of such...definitive, Milo Cain-like action—would meet up again with her daughter, The Evil Bitch Caitlyn Connelly.

It would likely happen sooner, rather than later. And when it did, Milo intended to be right here, comfortably ensconced in Mommy's head, from where he would be able to finish off the beautiful pain in his ass once and for all. Eliminating Caitlyn Connelly was the only thing he cared about now, and the one thing he intended to accomplish.

It was the one thing he *would* accomplish.

Assuming, of course, the old hag didn't get herself arrested for murder in the meantime.

34

Virginia tried to get her breathing—and her nerves—under control. She lifted Milo's still-warm head and slid the pillow back under it. Then she stood motionless. She knew she was wasting valuable time, that she should be getting the hell out of there as fast as she possibly could without arousing undue suspicion. The amount of time it would take for someone to discover Milo's dead body was limited, probably *very* limited, and every second wasted meant a greater likelihood of being caught and arrested.

But if she left now, she *would* arouse suspicion, she was sure of it. She was panting as though she had just stepped off a treadmill, and sweat trickled down her face in numerous tiny rivulets.

She breathed deeply, in and out, willing herself to calm down. And it worked. More or less. She tried to digest the implications of today's ugly business. Virginia Ayers was a murderer. Another human being had died by her hands. Not even just another human being, which would be bad enough, but her own child.

She had crossed a line and could never go back. And it wasn't like she expected to get away with killing Milo Cain. Quite the opposite. The minute a nurse or a doctor or a guard came in here and discovered Mr. Midnight's lifeless body, prison staff would immediately become suspicious. The inmate/patient dying right after being visited by his mother—the same mother who had now come two days in a row after being absent for six months—would raise red flags in the head of anyone but the densest of idiots. And Warden Ciuffetti struck Virginia as a lot of things, but idiotic wasn't among them.

An autopsy would be performed and Virginia had no doubt it would show Milo had been suffocated.

There would be only one suspect.

But none of that particularly concerned Virginia. She had taken the only action possible in a desperate attempt to protect her *other* child, and she knew that having done so, she would punish herself far worse every day for the rest of her life than the Commonwealth of Massachusetts ever could.

She would eventually be arrested, tried, and convicted of murder. She would serve out the rest of her days in prison. She might even become as notorious as Milo: the mother who cold-bloodedly executed her paralyzed and comatose son.

Wouldn't that be ironic.

Whatever the ultimate consequences, she accepted them. Looked forward to them, almost.

But not now. Not yet. She had to see Caitlyn one more time as a free woman, had to explain to her what she had been trying to do and how desperately she had wanted to help.

To give Caitlyn one last hug and tell her she loved her.

That was all she wanted. Then Massachusetts could have her. They could exact whatever punishment they deemed appropriate and Virginia would not fight them.

But not yet. Right now, she needed to make her way out of Bridgewater State Hospital and get on an airplane to Florida as quickly as she possibly could.

She considered the pressure in her skull and its significance. The odd sensation had leveled off, exactly as Caitlyn described to her. It was distracting for its unusual nature but not particularly painful. It was like having a head cold without the coughing or the sneezing or the runny nose. The painful thing was what it signified: the presence of Milo Cain.

Virginia decided she could live with it. For now. She had no choice.

She took one last deep breath and let it out slowly.

Wiped the sweat from her face with her sleeve.

And turned around to find the guard leveling his gun in her face.

"STEP AWAY FROM THE inmate," he said quietly. His voice was clear and his gun hand steady.

"Excuse me? What's the matter?" Virginia asked, wrinkling her brow, trying to look innocent, doubting she could pull it off. She didn't think she could ever look innocent again. It was a wasted effort. She had been caught and that was it. There would be no seeing Caitlyn again until she was behind bars. Still, she had to try.

"I watched you remove the pillow from the inmate's face, and then I watched you place it under his head. I'm not sure what's going on here, but know what it looks like. Now step away. I won't ask again."

Virginia had no choice. She did as she was told, moving toward the side wall.

The guard eased up to Milo's hospital bed. He shifted the gun from his right hand to his left but kept it pointed in Virginia's direction. Then he reached down and placed the first two fingers of his right hand lightly against Milo's neck, just under his ear.

For a moment nothing happened and then the guard's eyes narrowed and he looked over at Virginia incredulously. "He's dead. You killed him. You crazy bitch, you killed your own son. Nobody in the world is going to miss this sick son of a bitch, but *you killed your own son*." He shook his head. "I guess now I know where he got it from."

He shifted the gun back to his right hand and took one step toward Virginia. "Turn around and put your hands behind your back. You're coming with me."

Before she could comply, the man's body jerked once and became still. It was as though he had taken a jolt of electricity. His eyes glazed over and his facial expression slackened and he said woodenly, "You're free to go now, Ms. Ayers. Go straight to the exit and get out."

Milo.

Virginia's blood ran cold. *Oh, God, I've made things worse. I tried to help and I've only made things worse.* She prayed Milo wouldn't force the guard to injure or even kill himself just for fun. Her eyes filled with tears and she was paralyzed by fear. She literally could not move. She thought of Milo's useless body and recognized the irony.

Then the guard hissed, "I told you to leave, now *get out!*"

And Virginia had an epiphany. She had to do as she was told. She had to leave. The alternative was to disobey the guard/Milo and in doing so bring a bloodbath to Bridgewater State Hospital. Milo would force suggestions into the guard's brain, ugly suggestions, and soon the killing would start, and it would come from a guard, someone unexpected, and by the time it was all over, it would be like Milo had wrought the apocalypse.

And it would all be Virginia's fault.

So she began walking. She edged past the guard, who had lowered his gun and was now standing stock-still, like an appliance that had been unplugged. She tottered to the door, feeling like she might be sick to her stomach at any moment.

Looked back at the guard. He hadn't moved a muscle as far as she could tell.

She opened the door and forced what she hoped was a look of composure onto her face.

Then she walked out into the hallway, closing the door firmly behind her.

35

Getting out of the prison was easy. Virginia simply retraced her steps to the front entrance and walked out the door. She kept expecting to be challenged by someone, for a guard to come around a corner and ask brusquely what the hell an old lady was doing walking around a supposedly secure penitentiary unescorted.

But nothing of the kind happened. The few people she saw—a couple of harried nurses while she was still in the medical portion of the facility, and then a couple of guards after that—paid her no attention whatsoever.

She wondered whether that was Milo's doing or not. There was no way of knowing for sure, but her guess was that, while Milo wouldn't hesitate to take action if necessary to ensure her escape—it was obviously to his advantage to do so—the Bridgewater State Hospital staff was so shorthanded and so overworked that unless she brandished a weapon and shouted "Death to the pigs!" everyone was so busy with their own duties, they weren't about to add to their workload by worrying about one harmless old lady.

Ten minutes later she was out of the facility and sliding into the taxi, grateful she had paid the driver handsomely to wait for her.

"Where to now?" the bored cabbie asked.

She considered the question. Milo's "suggestions" to the guard would only hold for so long, and when they wore off, it would take almost no time at all for someone to discover the dead body lying in

Milo's room. Shortly after that, the authorities would begin looking for her.

And she wasn't quite ready to be apprehended yet. She had gotten a second chance from the last person in the world she would ever have expected to receive one, and even though Milo's reason for granting it were obviously diametrically opposed to hers, she wanted to make the most of that chance.

Having Milo inside her brain was terrifying, but Virginia was starting to work through the fear and the horror and thought that maybe, just maybe, there was a way to deal with the situation.

First things first, though. She had to get out of here.

"Providence, Rhode Island," she said. "T.F. Green State Airport."

The cabbie suddenly looked a lot less bored and a lot more pleased.

Virginia had lived in New England her entire life until moving to Tampa last fall, and she knew that Green Airport was actually located south of Providence, in Warwick, Rhode Island. So not only had the driver made good money to cool his heels in a Bridgewater parking lot, he was about to collect his second decent-sized fare of the day.

The cab accelerated out of the lot and turned toward Interstate 495. Virginia turned in her seat and watched the buildings of the ancient Bridgewater State Hospital complex shrink away to nothing through the rear window, her nerves settling but her mind still filled with conflicting emotions.

And Milo Cain.

SHE HAD CHOSEN GREEN Airport because she doubted the cabbie would be able to complete the roughly fifty-minute drive to Boston's Logan Airport before Milo's lifeless body was discovered.

Once that happened and the authorities began questioning her, she would never be able to hide her guilt. Nor would she attempt to. She was willing, even anxious, to accept the consequences of her actions. The time simply wasn't right yet.

The scenery whizzed past as the cab sped south, crossing the line from Massachusetts into Rhode Island. Virginia barely noticed. All her attention was focused on what was going to happen, or what probably already *was* happening, back in Bridgewater. Once Milo's lifeless body was discovered, the police would research Virginia's recent travel history, and then would dispatch an officer to Logan to intercept her before she could depart.

Green Airport was almost exactly the same distance from Bridgewater as Logan was, just in a different direction—not to mention a different state—so while there was some possibility they would cover that departure point as well, it seemed unlikely, for a couple of reasons.

First, no matter what their suspicions, it would take the authorities some time to determine with certainty that Milo's death following his mother's visit actually was murder and not just an odd coincidence. This would make Virginia Ayers simply a person of interest and not a murder suspect. This would likely make a critical difference in how thoroughly they searched for her.

For a while.

But even more importantly, Milo Cain had brutally tortured and murdered at least a dozen people in the Boston area over the last decade, and been responsible for the murder of a law enforcement officer in Revere last summer. His death would not exactly bring tears to anyone's eyes in Massachusetts. The initial reaction of the guard back at Bridgewater—*nobody in the world is going to miss this sick son of a bitch*—would be the reaction of police officials everywhere.

The murder would be investigated, of course it would, and Virginia would eventually face prosecution. But the amount of sweat equity expended by the authorities in tracking down Milo Cain's killer could not help but be affected by their revulsion to his gruesome personal history.

It might not be right or fair, but Virginia felt certain it was true. So she tried to relax as the taxi cruised through the city of Providence. She remained frightened as hell of the specter inside her head but only slightly of the police.

Soon they would reach T.F. Green airport, and shortly after that Virginia Ayers—and what was left of Milo Cain—would be airborne, headed back to the Gulf Coast of Florida and whatever fate awaited them there.

36

Milo would not have imagined it possible after spending the last six months trapped inside a smashed and motionless body, but he was bored out of his mind. Back in the first phase of his life, before that fateful afternoon in Revere when everything changed, Milo had spent every day living on a razor's edge.

For those existing on the fringes of society, life was sharper, clearer and more focused than for those comfortably ensconced in "normal" American society. "Normal" people's senses had long since been dulled by their warm, safe homes, and their reliable cars, and their steady paychecks, and their fully stocked refrigerators and 401(k)s.

"Normal" people walked around all day with their shields up but their guard down, convinced of their own invincibility for no good reason.

For people like Milo, the reality was the opposite. When you lived on the street, there was no opportunity to become soft if you expected to survive. Every day was a struggle, every meal's availability a questionable concept, each night's sleep restless and guarded.

A large percentage of the homeless population suffered from mental illness and/or addiction. But the ones who survived possessed an almost feral quality, an animal-like cunning. The rest were swallowed up quickly by the casual brutality of life on the street.

Milo had been far above the typical street person on the evolutionary chain. He suffered from no addictions, at least none of the chemical kind, and while he fully recognized that his unusual "hobby" was likely an indication of mental illness—sociopathy if not full-fledged psychopathy—he didn't consider that factor to be a negative.

Quite the opposite, in fact. Milo Cain had lived on the streets because he *chose* to live on the streets, not because he had no reasonable alternative. And what some would consider to be unhealthy choices—his compulsion to cut and stab and pierce and rend and watch in rapt fascination as the subjects of his ministrations eventually, inevitably, stopped breathing—Milo regarded as the ultimate proof of his advanced evolutionary state.

So, after prowling the streets and back alleys of Boston for so long, every day filled with life-and-death challenges, to wind up paralyzed in a hospital bed and lost inside his own head in a comatose state had been a torture worse than any he had perpetrated with blades and pliers on his unwilling victims. Milo had wished desperately for death, for a way out of the living hell that had become his existence.

Then everything changed. When he discovered his unique ability to *push* suggestions into people's brains, *and not only did the people accept the suggestions but then acted on them as well,* Milo had instantly discovered a new lease on life.

Discovering the ability to transport himself inside The Evil Bitch Caitlyn Connelly's head, though, was when he had truly started living again. To leave the dreary confines of Bridgewater State Hospital and his endless personal darkness behind was so liberating that it was almost as delectable as the realization he could still destroy The Evil Bitch's life and then, once she was out of the way, move on to bigger and better adventures.

So to be fortunate enough to escape his dying body and then take up residence inside the head of the person who had suffocated him should have been the adventure of a lifetime. Not only did the unlikely situation represent the ultimate opportunity for revenge, but it kept him here, on earth, where he would continue to wreak havoc.

But *this* wasn't the adventure of a lifetime. *This* was sheer torture. Riding in a taxi, heading to the airport—Providence, not Boston, a bit of misdirection the police would never expect from the old bird Virginia Ayers, and one for which his former status as a decade-long outlaw gave him an appreciation that would have been lost on most people—was just about the most uninteresting thing he could imagine.

On the other hand, this boring slice of middle-class travel hell gave Milo plenty of time to think. And that was something he desperately needed to do.

Because he had a problem. A big one.

He had escaped the destruction of his physical body through sheer dumb luck—with the lights going out he had done the only thing he could think of at the time—but while the result had been satisfactory, it represented at best no more than a temporary reprieve.

He was alive, if you could call it that, inside a sick old woman's head. She was not even sixty, but looked and acted decades older. And she was clearly on the downhill slide. There was no telling how long it would be before her heart simply exploded inside her old biddy chest.

And when she croaked, then what? The only heads he had been able to jump into were those of blood relatives: Caitlyn, his sister, and Virginia, his mother. He was committed with all his heart to the destruction of The Evil Bitch, so after he eliminated her, and then Mommy Dearest's physical deterioration was complete and her stain was finally removed from the earth, what would happen to Milo?

He chewed on the problem as the miles flew by. Soon they would arrive at the airport in Providence, and a couple of short hours after that they would be in Tampa.

Where Caitlyn was.

He couldn't wait to see Caitlyn. Couldn't wait to end her existence.

This was his dilemma. The smart move would be to swallow his hatred of her and allow her to live. Suck it up and deal with the unquenchable fury he felt whenever he saw her or even thought about her. By allowing Connelly to live, *he* could live on as well. It was the only reasonable strategy. Occupy Mommy Dearest's head until her inevitable end, and then jump into The Evil Bitch's skull when the old lady croaked.

There was only one problem with that strategy, but it was a big one. Potentially a deal breaker. Caitlyn Connelly made his skin crawl. From the very moment he had first laid eyes on her, Milo had despised the little bitch with an intensity that had shocked even him.

He hated everything about her, from her perfect skin to her lovely figure to her smug self-assurance to her success in life to her wannabe-hero boyfriend. Everything. He was certain if he knew more about her, he would hate those things, too.

The notion of spending several decades trapped inside *her* head was simply more than he could bear. It would drive him mad. It was unacceptable.

But if nothing else, Milo Cain had always been one adaptable motherfucker. Working the system was how he had lived his entire life, and he wasn't about to stop now.

There was an answer to this little conundrum, he was sure of it. All he had to do was keep working the issue and eventually the solution would present itself. It always had.

In the meantime, Milo was content to look out through the rheumy eyes of his murderer as she left Massachusetts behind and made her escape. The old broad had shown a lot more gumption than he would ever have given her credit for, and while he couldn't say he was exactly happy to have had the life choked out of him by his own mother, it was an eye-opening experience, no pun intended.

After more than thirty years walking this earth, most of it feeling as unconnected to the rest of the human race as an alien from outer space, Milo had finally learned where he had picked up his penchant for killing.

From Dear Old Mom.

37

Cait barely noticed the phone when it started ringing. The sound was irrelevant, like the buzzing of a mosquito just as she was about to fall asleep, back in the days when she actually *could* sleep.

She was still seated at her kitchen table. She tried to figure out how long she had been zoned out here and realized she couldn't. But that was fine, because what difference did it make, anyway?

An old rock album her adoptive dad used to listen to flashed into her head. It was by John Mellencamp and was titled *Nothin' Matters and What If It Did?* She was starting to understand the sentiment.

The phone continued to ring and Cait continued not to answer it. After the prescribed six rings, the answering machine clicked on and Cait heard herself say, "Kevin and I are either not here or too busy to get to the phone right now. Please leave a message, and we'll call you back as soon as we can. Unless you're a telemarketer, in which case, go away and don't call back."

The message made her heart ache, as did just about everything else in this apartment. She had recorded the message with Kevin sitting next to her goading her on. He laughed like hell when she added the business about the telemarketers, because it had been so unlike her. Uptight lawyer chick telling the telemarketers off.

Now, as she listened, Cait made a mental note to change the message. It reminded her too much of Kevin to leave it. Maybe she would simply unplug the damn answering machine, ignore the phone, and hope people would eventually get tired of calling and leave her alone.

Right now, though, the machine rolled through its spiel and after the beep, Cait heard the voice of her mother through the tinny speaker. She sounded tired, stressed. "Hello, Caitlyn, are you there, honey? Please pick up if you are."

She sighed and pushed back from the table. She reached for the phone and glanced at the clock, shocked to discover she had been sitting immobile for more than three hours. Her back ached. Her knees cracked as she stood.

She picked up the phone. "Hello?" Her voice sounded hollow and uninterested, even to her.

"Hello, dear, how are you doing?"

"I'm fine," she answered automatically. "How's your visit going?"

There was a short pause and then Virginia said, "I'm on my way home. Remember I told you I'd call you from the airplane?"

"Oh. Yeah." The conversation came back to her now. It felt as though it had taken place a hundred years ago. She was exhausted but couldn't sleep, worried about Kevin but unable to do a damn thing to help him. She wondered if she would ever get a truly good night's sleep again.

She remembered her mother asking for a ride home from the airport and she said, "What time will you be arriving in Tampa?"

"I'm not flying into Tampa. I'll be landing at Sarasota in exactly two hours, as long as the flight doesn't get delayed."

"Sarasota? Why aren't you coming into Tampa? Couldn't you get a flight?"

"It's complicated," she said. "I'll explain everything when I see you."

"Uh...okay," Cait said, looking at the clock again and trying to figure out how long it would take to get to Sarasota-Bradenton International Airport. It was a minor relief just to be able to think about something mundane for a few seconds. "I'll have plenty of time to make it to the airport before your arrival."

"No, honey, I've changed my mind. You sound like someone who's been up for forty-eight hours. I want you to get some rest. I'll take a cab from the airport and come straight to your apartment. We can talk then."

Cait blinked tiredly. Her eyes felt scratchy and her mouth dry, and she realized her mother's forty-eight hours comment wasn't all that far off. "No, Mom, I want to come and pick you up. I need to get out. It'll be good to have something to do, and I'm fine to drive, I promise. I'll grab a coffee on the way and I'll be good as new."

Virginia blew out a breath. It was clear she was unconvinced. "I suppose," she said, "but if you change your mind, just text me. Taking a cab would be absolutely no problem."

That wasn't going to happen. She agreed to let her mother know if she changed her mind, only to ease her concerns. But now that she had said it, Cait really did believe that she needed to get out, to get moving, to *do* something, even if it was something as simple as driving to Sarasota and back. It might not make her feel better, and it *certainly* wasn't going to make her any less frightened—she doubted the fear would ever go away until Milo finally got what he wanted and put her in the ground—but sitting at her kitchen table like an extra from *Night of the Living Dead* wasn't accomplishing anything, either.

She hung up the phone and sat for another minute, elbows on the table, chin in her hands. Then she got up with a sigh and started getting ready to go out.

38

Virginia stared at her cell phone for a long time after hanging up with Cait. Her daughter sounded nothing like the person she had gotten to know so well over the last six months. Following the violent confrontation with Milo Cain last summer, during which Cait had been brutalized and disfigured, Virginia had wondered whether her personality would be forever altered.

But although she had suffered through painful skin grafts and a long and still-ongoing recovery, Cait had for the most part responded well. Bouts of insomnia came and went, as did the occasional nightmare, but Caitlyn had focused on her career and her relationship with Kevin, and her basic optimistic nature had remained intact.

This was different. By focusing his destructive power on Kevin, Milo had wounded Cait in the worst possible way. Her physical injuries were relatively minor, at least compared to last summer, but having to watch her lover's life and career be torn apart was devastating to her.

And she blamed herself. She was adrift, wracked by guilt and tortured by fear. She was convinced Milo Cain would not stop until he had ruined everything in her life and then killed her, and nothing Virginia had seen to this point had given her any reason to question Caitlyn's theory.

Hence, Virginia's visit to Bridgewater State Hospital and her attempt to solve the problem, an attempt that had only complicated matters even more.

But although Virginia knew Milo was lurking inside her head, waiting like a coiled cobra to strike, she knew also that as much as he sometimes seemed omnipotent, he most certainly was not. Maybe he could latch onto her sight like some kind of human leech to see the world through her eyes, but he could not read her mind. He could not know what she was thinking or planning.

In a way, this morning's trip to Bridgewater had been liberating. She would never be able to overcome the grief and revulsion she felt at suffocating her own child while he lay alone and helpless, chained to a hospital bed, but she was comfortable with her decision. At peace. She would do whatever it took to protect Caitlyn.

The muted hum of a dozen individual conversations wafted around Virginia as the plane cruised straight and level down the East Coast. Her concern about what Milo might do next, what suggestion he might decide to push into some innocent bystander's head just for fun was tempered with her certainty of his one overriding aim: to destroy his twin sister.

To that end, he was not about to direct the pilots to fly the plane into the ground, or to force a passenger to leap out of his seat and attack a flight attendant, holding a pen to her throat while screaming that he was hijacking the plane to Cuba. None of those things would get him any closer to realizing his goal, and Milo Cain was nothing if not dogged and single-minded.

So for now, Virginia felt no particular anxiety. That would change when she got on the ground in Florida, of course, especially if Cait kept to her word and drove out to Sarasota to pick her up. Then things might get dicey.

But Virginia had been using her anonymity and the solitude of the Boeing 757, three-quarters filled with strangers, to do a lot of thinking. She was starting to believe she had a pretty good handle on Milo's destructive new abilities, the ones he had only developed since being shot in the face.

Her first and most obvious theory regarding her son was that whatever psychic wavelength Milo was using to push suggestions into people's heads was useless when dealing with his own bloodline. It had to be true, otherwise he would simply have pushed a suggestion into Cait's head that she kill herself and been done with it.

The intensity with which Milo hated his twin sister left no room for doubt on that score. If he could have forced her death by her own hand, he would have done so. This also explained why he wouldn't have simply implanted a suggestion into *Virginia's* mind to kill Cait. They spent so much time together now that it would have been a simple thing to do.

If he could have.

As the plane floated south, oblivious passengers dozing or reading or chatting or watching a movie, Virginia mulled over the precious few bits of information she possessed. She looked at them from as many different angles as she could conceive and tried to think the way Milo Cain would think, as awful as that seemed.

And she began developing a plan. She didn't know much, but it might be just enough to allow her to take action. It would be up to her to end the nightmare and, in so doing, protect Caitlyn. No one else could do it.

On reflection, that seemed only fair. Fitting. She had birthed Milo Cain and, in so doing, unleashed his evil on the world, however unwittingly. It would fall to her to put a stop to it.

And she now knew how she would do it.

The Boeing 757 began descending, the skies so smooth the drop in altitude was almost imperceptible. But Virginia could feel it. The implications of that descent were huge. Soon they would be on the ground in Florida and for better or worse she would put her hastily devised plan in motion.

It wasn't complicated. In Virginia's experience, the best courses of action never were. In fact, her plan was damned simple. There weren't many details. But she used the rapidly evaporating time to chew at those details like a dog worrying a bone.

She was playing with fire; she knew that. All of her theories regarding Milo Cain's destructive abilities were just that—theories. Milo was inside her head now, with no body, no physical anchor, no place else to go. He was like a deadly cancer in her brain, waiting to strike, but instead of inflicting suffering on her, he could lash out from her head at anyone she spoke to or looked at as they passed on the street.

He was a ticking time bomb. If her theories about what he could and could not do were wrong, even if she misjudged just a little, the result could be a barrage of devastation and suffering more horrifying than anything she could imagine.

But she had to try. She was inextricably linked to one of the most dangerous and frightening men in America, and she was the only person alive who even stood a chance of bringing his reign of terror to a close.

If only she could reach inside and summon the courage her plan would require.

39

Virginia pulled her wheeled suitcase behind her as she walked through the terminal building. The sense of calm she experienced on board the flight from Massachusetts had vanished, disappearing in the knowledge of how much damage Milo could do in this crowd of people if he chose to.

She spotted Cait almost immediately upon exiting the jetway. Even though she had known her daughter was depressed and exhausted from the earlier phone call, she recoiled in surprise at exactly *how* depressed and exhausted she looked. Cait's face was pale and drawn, and she moved with the tired, deliberate motions of someone twice her age.

She looks like me.

The thought sprang into her head unbidden and she shuddered. She was well aware of the link between her own physical deterioration and the family tragedies she had endured, and it broke her heart to see the same thing happening to Caitlyn.

I'm going to fix this, she thought. She wanted to scream it to her beautiful child but didn't. Instead, she rushed forward, keeping her gaze focused on Caitlyn and Caitlyn only. She wrapped her arms around her daughter in a bear hug and squeezed her eyes shut, ignoring as best she could the throng of travelers bumping and jostling them as they passed.

Cait's chest heaved and Virginia realized she was sobbing. "We'll get through this," she whispered, wishing she could explain her plan but knowing that for it to have any chance of success—even as minimal as that chance undoubtedly was—her only advantage over Milo was surprise, and she could lose that in a heartbeat.

Caitlyn shook her head in silent rejection of Virginia's promise. "What have you done?" she said, the words quiet and hollow.

Virginia didn't understand the question but didn't care right now; she wanted the hug to go on forever. At last she gave one final squeeze and whispered, "It's good to see you again." She felt silly saying it because they had only been apart for a day, but she was only now beginning to understand how precious time was.

After what felt simultaneously like hours and the blink of an eye, Virginia released her grip, stepping back and smiling at Cait. "Let's get out of here," she said, and began walking briskly toward the terminal's exit.

MILO HAD BEEN CAUGHT off guard when Mommy Dearest exited the plane and almost immediately spotted The Evil Bitch in the crowd. He didn't know why, he should have been expecting exactly that since it was what they had agreed to when they spoke on the phone.

But he was feeling logy, tired, like he badly needed a nap. He recalled the extreme exhaustion that had followed on the heels of his previous trips into Caitlyn Connelly's head and wondered whether this was the same thing. He had assumed that the elimination of his physical being would eliminate physical sensations like exhaustion, but perhaps that was not the case. Perhaps even though his body was gone and he was now fully an ethereal being, he was still subject to some of the old physical constraints.

Regardless, it was a subject for consideration at another time, because no sooner had Virginia Ayers locked eyes with Caitlyn Connelly than the old familiar rage began to bubble. No matter how hard he tried to control it, no matter how often he told himself to be rational, to think things through, he simply could not contain his hatred for his twin, who had been so fortunate in the genetic lottery at *his* expense.

His exhaustion receded and he began to contemplate all the deliciously depraved things he would like to do to pretty little Caitlyn Connelly. Should he end her now? Should he get this depressing chapter of his story over with so he could finally move on to bigger and better things?

Mommy Dearest embraced The Evil Bitch and Milo felt sick to his stomach. The fact that he no longer had a stomach to be sick to was irrelevant. These two stupid bitches were the cause of all his pain, and he had been saddled with them—or at least with one of them—irrevocably.

No wonder he was bitter. No wonder he was angry. No wonder he wanted to cut and slice and rend and stab, until Caitlyn Connelly was nothing more than a piece of bloody meat lying dead on the floor of the terminal building, no more recognizable as human than a pile of rotting meat.

This was it.

He would kill her now. He couldn't wait any longer.

It was an easy decision, really, and he relished the opportunity to end things.

This would be child's play. Even though they were inside an airline terminal where, ostensibly, weapons were banned, Milo knew that would make little difference. He wouldn't need a conventional weapon like a gun or a knife. He could make almost anything into a lethal killing device.

And as much as he would have loved the opportunity to carve up sis one final time, for old time's sake if nothing else, he had grown so sick of her and so tired of her Goody-Two-Shoes act that simply ridding the world of her would be satisfying enough.

He gazed through the tired old eyes of Virginia Ayers, looking for someone to push a suggestion into. Someone to bend to his will.

But the stupid old biddy wasn't looking around the terminal. In fact, she wasn't *looking* at all! Her goddamned eyes were closed as she hugged The Evil Bitch tight and whispered sweet nothings into her ear.

The fury that he had worked so hard to contain built nearly to the exploding point as Milo waited for Mommy Dearest to open her eyes. All he would need would be a few seconds, for Virginia to look around the crowded terminal, and he knew he'd be able to find something—and someone—he could use as a weapon. A blunt instrument.

But she had to open her eyes.

Finally she did and Milo breathed a little easier, although of course he wasn't really breathing at all. Virginia stepped back and looked into The Evil Bitch's face. Tears were running down Connelly's cheeks, smearing mascara and making her look like a fucking circus clown, and Milo would have laughed out loud if he could have.

The old biddy stared at Connelly for what felt like forever and then at last she shifted her gaze elsewhere as she began walking toward the exit. Milo watched expectantly through her eyes, ready to pounce at the first opportunity.

But then the anger began to swell again, building and building and there was nothing he could do about it, no way he could release it. *Virginia wasn't looking at anyone!* She stared resolutely at the floor as she walked, locking eyes with no one, not even looking at where she was going.

She bumped into people and murmured apologies but stared at the floor. She nearly tripped over a seeing-eye dog, stumbling and almost falling flat on her face, jostling the blind guy but still refusing to look up. The blind guy swore and Virginia apologized again but kept going, gaze still focused straight down at the tops of her stumbling feet.

Out of the corner of her eye, Milo saw her grab Connelly's hand. She said, "Lead me to the car," and when The Evil Bitch asked what was wrong, she said nothing.

Connelly stopped for a moment and the old biddy stopped right behind her. Finally Virginia said, "I'll explain everything later, but for now, please, Caitlyn, just get us to your car."

The tension was plain in her voice and for a second nothing happened. Then they started moving again and Milo knew the dried-up old crone was fucking with him. She knew he was inside her head, probably had known it ever since the guard allowed her to escape custody at Bridgewater State Hospital. She had figured out somehow that he could make people do things against their will, and was intentionally stymying him, knowing he would wanted nothing more than to waste Caitlyn Connelly.

Rather than increasing his already simmering fury, this insight actually calmed Milo, if only slightly. If Mommy Dearest wanted to play games, he would play games. She had no fucking idea who she was playing with. Milo Cain had been strategizing and manipulating people in deadly mind games virtually his entire life. He had been living on the street, fucking with innocent victims while she was eating TV dinners and watching Jeopardy! every night, reading romance novels and pretending to have a life.

You want to play, bitch? Bring it on.

She could stare at the floor all she wanted, it wouldn't do a goddamned bit of good. She could stumble into people and be dragged around by The Evil Bitch until hell froze over and it wouldn't make a damned bit of difference.

Because eventually she would have to look into the face of someone who wasn't Caitlyn Connelly. Eventually she would interact with someone else—a pizza delivery guy, or a bus driver, or a police officer, or any other fucking person on the planet.

And when she did, Milo would be there. And he would take over then and do what he did best. He would be with Virginia Ayers until her fucking heart stopped, and sometime before then—probably well before then, probably sometime today, in fact—she would give him the opening he needed.

And it would only take a moment.

40

In addition to being caught in the grip of a depression unlike any she had ever experienced, Cait was now confused and afraid. She was in the habit of listening to Tampa's News Radio WFLA in her car, and on the way to the airport the scheduled broadcast had been interrupted by a special breaking-news report: notorious serial torturer/murderer Milo Cain had been found dead in his bed at Bridgewater State Hospital in Massachusetts.

Authorities weren't releasing any details, but as far as Cait was concerned, they didn't have to. Suddenly, her mother's abrupt decision to stay in Boston one extra night made perfect, awful sense.

Virginia hadn't been going to visit an old neighborhood friend at all. She had been driven to the end of her rope by Milo's brand of chaos and destruction, exactly as Cait had. But instead of hiding away in her apartment, lost and hopeless, Virginia Ayers had decided to put an end to the madness once and for all.

Suddenly, everything was clear. The extra overnight stay. The obfuscation when Cait had asked her about her plans. The flight into Sarasota instead of Tampa. She had known the authorities would be looking for her almost the minute she left the hospital/prison, so she had crossed them up by flying somewhere other than Tampa to come home.

Cait's head spun. Virginia had gone to the Bridgewater facility one last time and had killed Milo in his bed.

She had gone against her own moral code and risked her own freedom to save Cait's life.

Now, Cait would lose not just Kevin, but her mother as well, just a few short months after finally finding her and establishing a relationship. To know her birth mother was all she had ever wanted and now she was going to lose the connection she had given up so much to forge. She wanted to scream, to cry, to grab her mother by the arms and shake her and ask what the hell she thought she was doing.

But she couldn't do any of that, at least not now and not here.

And Virginia was acting very strangely. After that first intense gaze into Cait's eyes, her mother had directed her gaze downward, like a shy child, and had refused to look up, not even to see where she was going. When she grabbed Cait's hand and instructed her to lead the way to the car, Cait had complied mostly out of utter shock.

The last few minutes had been surreal, and that was saying something given the nightmare that Cait's life had become. They walked through the concrete parking garage, their footsteps echoing loudly in the relative cool of the multi-story structure, moving slowly as Cait was forced to lead Virginia by the hand.

They passed other travelers and Virginia steadfastly refused to look at them.

They walked up a set of concrete stairs and while Virginia released her grip on Cait's hand to clutch the iron rail as they climbed, she still stared resolutely downward and then grabbed Cait's hand like a drowning woman reaching for a life preserver the moment they reached the top.

Cait asked again what was the matter and again she refused to answer. "Not now," she said.

Finally they reached Cait's car and she pressed the remote to unlock the vehicle. She guided Virginia to the passenger door and helped her inside, then hefted her mother's suitcase and placed it in the backseat.

When she had slid into the driver's seat, Cait looked over at her mother to see that she had lifted her head and was looking back at her with red-rimmed, watery eyes. "I'm so sorry," she said.

CAIT WAS UNFAMILIAR with the area immediately surrounding Sarasota-Bradenton International Airport, so once they had exited the parking garage, she forced herself to hold off asking any questions. Instead, she concentrated on navigating to I-75.

Virginia sat silently next to her. She had closed her mouth and said nothing more after her tearful apology, and Cait noticed immediately that her mother continued the strange behavior she had exhibited at the airport. She looked either directly at Cait or kept her gaze dashboard-level or below. Never did she lift her eyes to look out the windshield or the side window.

Once they had turned north toward Tampa and merged with traffic, Cait said softly, "You killed Milo, didn't you?"

Her mother opened her mouth as if to speak. Then she closed it.

She opened it again and breathed in deeply. Closed it again.

When she looked over at Cait, her eyes indicated a hopelessness more complete than any Cait had ever seen. They were haunted. Desolate. "I was trying to save you from this living hell I brought on you," she said. "It was the only thing I could think of to do."

The tears that Cait felt had become a permanent part of her reality now welled to the surface once again. "You didn't bring anything on me. In fact, it was just the opposite. I brought all of this on myself, and on you as well. You knew what would happen if I insisted on pursuing my dream of learning my family history, tried to warn me, in fact. But I wouldn't listen, and now I've destroyed the lives of the very people I wanted to love the most."

Virginia began shaking her head halfway through Cait's statement and didn't stop until she had finished speaking. "No, honey, who in your circumstances would *not* have wanted to learn her history, to find out why she was given up when she was just a day old? It was my fault for not being stronger and refusing to call you back last summer when Milo was torturing me. A few more minutes and your plane would have been in the air, and maybe everything would have been different."

"But Milo would have killed you."

"Maybe that would have been for the best," Virginia whispered.

The car fell silent for a moment and Cait said fiercely, "It would *not* have been for the best. Getting to know my mother has been worth every bit of heartache I've gone through, but I'll regret forever what I brought on you and Kevin. But that's water under the bridge, and all we can do is move forward from here. Milo's gone now and he can't hurt anyone ever again."

"Listen, Caitlyn..."

"Let me finish. I mentioned moving forward, and if we're going to do so, we have a lot to think about. The authorities either are looking for you now or will be soon, that much is obvious. You're going to have to turn yourself in because you have no other reasonable option."

"Please, Caitlyn, let me—"

"I have to say this, Mom. When I've said my piece, we can discuss everything, I promise, but right now I have to get this out. So here it is: I know you would never hurt a fly unless you felt you absolutely had no choice. I know you would never end the life of your own flesh and blood—even someone as intrinsically evil as Milo—unless you felt you absolutely had no choice.

"I know you did what you did to save me.

"I've been thinking about this nonstop, ever since hearing the radio report about Milo's death on my way over here. I understand why you did what you did and I think other people will, too, at least to a certain degree. They'll never understand Milo's ability to push suggestions while in a coma, or to take up residence in my head, of course. But still, I believe strongly that we can get you out of this. I have plenty of contacts in the legal community. I know several of the best criminal-defense attorneys in the state of Florida, and I'm willing to pay whatever their fees might be to secure their representation for you.

"I can't begin to imagine the pain you must be feeling, having no choice but to end your own child's life, but we have to look at this objectively. You didn't cold-bloodedly murder an innocent child, or even an innocent adult, for that matter. The man whose life you ended was one of the most feared and reviled people in modern American history, and not many—maybe not *any*—people are going to miss him."

She looked at her mother and Virginia was staring back, tears running freely down her face. "I'm sorry, Mom, I don't mean to be harsh. I know I'm talking about your son. He was my brother, too, but he was irreparably broken, both physically and emotionally. You know that better than anyone, probably. And his status as a serial murderer *will* play a part in any jury's consideration of the charges you'll face.

"When that fact is combined with your ill health, I believe there's every reason to expect you will receive a minimal sentence. With a little luck and the right jury, you might even receive nothing harsher than probation.

"But the important thing to remember is we're in this together, just as Kevin and I are going to be in it together, too, now that Milo can't hurt us anymore. I'm going to support you as much as I can for as long as it takes. The three of us are a family and we'll get through whatever comes next by sticking together."

Virginia sniffled and opened Cait's glove box. She removed a tissue and wiped the tears from her cheeks. She sniffled again and said, "Thank you so much for your understanding, honey, I don't think there's any way I can express how much it means to me. But there's something you don't know, and it changes everything."

Cait looked across the front of the vehicle at her mother, puzzled. "What don't I know that could possibly change everything?"

"Milo's still here."

41

Milo thought there must have been some occurrence in his life that had been worse than being stuck inside a car with the two people he hated more than everyone else in the world put together, but at the moment he couldn't imagine what that might have been.

The closest he could come was when The Evil Bitch had shot him in the face at point-blank range. That had been a black day, to say the least. But everything had worked out better than he could possibly have hoped at the time. Not only had he survived the vicious attack, he had come through it even stronger and more powerful than before. Sure, his physical being had been damaged beyond repair, but the trade-off, and what he had gained, had been well worth it.

Setting aside that awful occurrence in Mommy Dearest's sitting room, Milo felt he had been pretty damned fortunate in life. He had lived the way he wanted, hunting among the defenseless and unsuspecting sheep for years and taking his pleasures from them pretty much whenever he damn well pleased.

So, on reflection, *this* definitely was the worst, most frustrating punishment he could possibly imagine enduring. Looking out through the old biddy's rheumy eyes as she stared resolutely at the dashboard or, even worse, The Evil Bitch, was bad enough.

But having to listen as they relentlessly besmirched his memory, trashing his reputation in the worst possible way just hours after snuffing out his physical presence, well, Milo thought that might be more than he could bear.

But of course, he had no choice in the matter. He *had* to bear it. The only alternative would be to jump from the old biddy's head into The Evil Bitch's head, and what the hell would that accomplish? Absolutely nothing. He would be no better off than before, stuck helplessly listening as they performed their relentless and undeserved character assassination on him.

And the worst part was that Milo knew without a shadow of a doubt the old biddy was aware of his presence. She had to know he could hear every word, and that their pathetic little display of family bonding would do nothing more than make the inevitable ending to this little drama that much more painful for the both of them.

And inevitable it was.

It was preordained.

There was only one way this silent standoff, Milo versus Virginia, *could* end: Eventually Mommy Dearest would forget, even for just a second, that she couldn't risk looking at or interacting with anyone except Caitlyn Connelly. Eventually she would do exactly that and when she did, Milo would take full advantage. He would strike without any semblance of mercy, not that he wouldn't have done so, anyway.

He half listened to them drone on, two hens clucking at each other inside their moving henhouse, as he daydreamed about the rapidly approaching end of The Evil Bitch's life. He would crush her like the bug that she was, and of course Mommy Dearest would be forced to watch, because *he* wanted to watch.

Then, after she had been disposed of, Milo would turn his attention and advanced brainpower on the issue of how he was going to escape Virginia Ayers's deteriorating body and into whose he was going to jump. The situation right now seemed hopeless—there was no reason to believe he *could* jump into anyone else's head—but Milo knew that once he focused his particular brand of advanced intelligence on the problem, a solution would present itself.

Perhaps he would push a suggestion into someone's brain to research the entire genealogical history of Virginia Ayers's family. It wouldn't be difficult. Hell, with the advent of the Internet, very little about researching *any* topic was difficult now.

Once the family tree was laid out in front of him like a road atlas, Milo was willing to bet that another suitable host would be found, someone blood-related closely enough to the old biddy that that person would have no choice but to serve as reluctant host.

Hell, if he played his cards right, Milo thought there was every possibility he might just be able to achieve near-immortality! Jump into the head of someone young enough to serve as his portal into the outside world for many decades, and then, as that person's life span ticked down, do another search and find another blood relative and start the entire process over again.

He smiled to himself. In the span of less than thirty minutes, while the two doomed women discussed his failings and their supposed superiority, Milo had solved his only real problem, and overcome the only barrier to his ascendance to near-Godlike status.

They still had no idea who they were fucking with. But they would find out soon enough.

THE EVIL BITCH'S CAR rolled down the highway—at least, Milo assumed it rolled down the highway, since he had no way of knowing for sure until the old biddy came to the inevitable realization that her stupid "plan" for stopping him was just as doomed as she was—and the women continued their pathetic love-fest, complimenting each other on their bravery and plotting ways to keep Mommy Dearest out of jail.

It was sickening, but their words became almost a tuneless buzzing to Milo as he made every effort to avoid paying too much attention to them. It was the only way he could keep from being overcome by self-righteous fury.

So he almost missed it when the old biddy revealed her secret to The Evil Bitch. Their words had been flowing over his consciousness like river water bubbling over a streambed, but somewhere inside, Milo's subconscious must have been paying attention because a half second after Virginia said the words, Milo shook off his lethargy and began concentrating.

Three little words he had never expected her to say; at least not to The Evil Bitch: "Milo's still here."

The fact that she spilled the beans didn't worry Milo. It didn't change anything to have Connelly know the truth. In fact, in some ways it made the situation even better. The terror The Evil Bitch would have to endure before Milo finished her off would be much deeper, more visceral, with the knowledge that he had not perished in Virginia's brutal display of treachery. She would suffer. And that knowledge would have warmed Milo's heart if he'd had one.

Still, this was an unexpected development, not just for him but for The Evil Bitch as well. The car veered violently to the right before Connelly wrestled the steering wheel the other direction, pulling the car back into its travel lane amidst the blaring of a pair of horns, one behind Connelly's car and one next to it.

They came damned close to dying, and wouldn't that have been ironic? In her panic, Mommy Dearest forgot her self-imposed prohibition on looking out the windshield, and Milo caught a glimpse of the silver iron guardrail rushing at them and then receding. Then the old biddy came to her senses and once again resumed staring at the dashboard.

A shocked silence pervaded the car's interior. This was getting interesting. Milo waited patiently, curious to see what would happen next.

42

Cait struggled to get the car back under control as the impact of her mother's words struck her with the force of a blow to the head. The familiar terror came rushing back, unreasoning and all encompassing, and for a moment it was all she could do to breathe.

She concentrated on keeping the car centered now that she had wrestled it back into its travel lane, only dimly aware she had nearly killed both herself and Virginia with her spastic reaction to the last words she had ever expected to hear out of her mother's mouth. Angry drivers honked at her and she ignored them.

For what felt like a long time, no one spoke. Then, when she thought she might be able to get the words out without advertising her terror too plainly, she said, "What do you mean, Milo's still here? The news reports were very specific. 'Milo Cain, notorious Boston serial torturer/murderer, was found dead in his bed at Bridgewater State Hospital outside of Boston today.' That was the report. Are you telling me that's a lie?"

Cait waited for her mother to answer, dreading what she might say. She prayed she had misheard the words, or misunderstood them, but knew at the same time she had not. She began to think Virginia was not *going* to answer, that she had played a hideously cruel practical joke on Cait for some unfathomable reason.

Then her mother answered, and the reality of the words was even worse than anything Cait could have dreamed in her most fevered nightmare. "No," she said. "The news reports were not a lie. And they were accurate, at least as far as they went."

"As far as they went." Cait shivered, although the temperature in her car had to be close to eighty degrees. "What is that supposed to mean?"

Virginia sighed. Cait thought the sound was filled with fear and regret and maybe even resignation. "It means there's more to the story. It means that while I did end Milo's physical life..."

The icy chill that had caused her to shiver began taking over Cait's body like an advancing army as Virginia spoke, leading the way for a sense of black dread that followed in its wake. It covered Cait like a blanket, trapping her beneath, alone with her terror as her mother finished speaking.

"It means," Virginia continued, "that while I did end Milo's physical life, he managed to find a way to survive outside his body."

Understanding began to dawn in Cait and with it, acceptance. The nightmare truly would never be over until she was dead. She had allowed herself the brief, plainly delusional hope that everything might finally be all right, but everything was not going to be all right. Everything would never be all right.

Cait knew now what Virginia was going to say, but she could no more interrupt her mother before she had finished speaking than she could perform surgery on herself or stop the sun from rising and setting every day.

"It means," Virginia finished, "that your head is not the only one Milo can leap into. I discovered that he can enter mine as well. I learned this the hard way. For both of us." Her voice faded away as she spoke until by the time she had finished her statement it was no more than a paper-thin whisper. The words floated into the air and disappeared like steam from a coffee cup.

But to Cait they may as well have been shouted through a megaphone or screamed from the top of a mountain.

Virginia's words contained a finality that could never be undone. It occurred to Cait that up until a moment ago, even when things had been at their worst—Kevin attacking his attorney inside the courtroom, for example—she had held on to a vague unreasoning hope, like a child wishing away the monster under the bed.

Not anymore. Not only was the monster still under the bed, it was now slithering/crawling/climbing out, mouth open, teeth exposed, ready to slash into her and devour her whole.

"He's here now, isn't he?" she said. Somewhere in a corner of her mind, Cait was surprised at how calm she sounded. Inside, she was a quivering, shaking little girl, stunned by the realization there would be no fairy-tale finish to her story. No prince was going to ride in on a white horse and save her at the last minute. Her prince was sitting in a jail cell and was unlikely to walk free for a long, long time.

"Yes," her mother said simply.

And everything made perfect, horrible sense. The words her mother had spoken last summer as they sat at her scarred, ancient kitchen table, about twins in the family's bloodline and one's inevitable violent end at the hands of the other weren't just history, static and immutable.

They were much more than that. They were a prophecy, living and breathing just as Cait lived and breathed herself. And she could never outrun that prophecy. She'd been a fool even to try.

"What happens now?" Cait asked, and she noticed the same tone of resignation in her words that she had sensed in her mother's sigh a few moments ago.

Virginia didn't answer, and Cait took her eyes off the road for just a second. She glanced over and blinked in surprise, unable to comprehend the sight: Virginia Ayers reaching for the door handle as the car hurtled along I-75 at nearly seventy miles per hour.

43

Virginia realized there was nothing more to say. There was plenty she *wanted* to say; she would have been happy to sit in the car talking with Caitlyn forever.

Their conversation, although centering on murders and jury trials and comatose family members with bizarre powers and homicidal tendencies, still felt as close to a normal mother/daughter conversation as she was ever likely to get, considering their tragic and violent family history.

As far as Virginia was concerned, Caitlyn could have driven to the Gulf of Mexico and then turned north, motoring on up west coast of Florida and then turning toward Nevada or California, or anywhere else far, far away. She wouldn't have minded a bit. They could talk and bond, just the two of them.

But it wasn't going to happen. They were getting dangerously close to Caitlyn's Tampa exit, and any mention by Virginia of passing the exit would be sure to raise the suspicions of Milo, who continued to lurk inside Virginia's head like a ticking time bomb.

She knew what she had to do and for it to be successful, Virginia had to do it while on the highway.

Hopefully Caitlyn would understand.

Virginia kept her gaze focused on the dashboard, exactly as she had done throughout the drive, with the only exceptions being the few occasions she looked into her daughter's eyes and the second or two of sheer panic when it seemed the car was about to smash into the guardrail.

It wasn't easy. One slip-up and Milo would tumble to what was happening, and then all would be lost.

She stared at the dashboard.

She carried on the conversation with her daughter regarding her son, making every effort not to sound any more stressed or upset than she had during the entire ride.

And she fumbled for the latch on her seat belt.

It was on her left side, the side closest to Caitlyn, and that was a problem. If Caitlyn noticed what she was doing, her natural reaction would be exactly the same as anyone else's: she would ask what in the hell was going on.

And that would be all it would take to raise Milo's suspicions.

So she worked slowly, deliberately, sliding her right hand across her body at her waist, doing her best to keep her hand and arm out of Caitlyn's peripheral vision.

Goddammit, this is hard.

With her left hand she braced the metal buckle, wrapping her small fist around it to deaden the sound as much as possible. Then she felt around the edge with her right hand, hooking her fingers under the latch.

She paused and took a deep breath, amazed she had managed to carry on an intelligent enough conversation to avoid raising the suspicions of Caitlyn or Milo. She hoped.

She pulled on the edge of the latch. It lifted maybe half an inch and then Virginia felt resistance. Then there was a small *click.* It sounded like a bomb exploding to Virginia and she froze, wanting desperately to glance up at Caitlyn to see whether she had noticed, but not daring to do so.

A second passed. Another. Caitlyn continued to drive and talk as though nothing had changed. Virginia breathed a sigh of relief. The seat belt was now unbuckled.

Keeping her eyes downcast as she had done all along, Virginia feigned a stretch, lifting her torso off the back of the seat and raising her arms. She slipped the reinforced strap of the restraint off her shoulder and at the same time leaned back, hoping to trap the belt against the seat before it could reel itself into place with the distinctive snapping sound anyone who has ever ridden in a car would recognize.

Again she held her breath, certain that her luck would run out and her desperate plan would be exposed.

Again nothing happened. Caitlyn continued on, unaware of her mother sitting next to her sliding out of her restraint like a naughty child.

Virginia knew she had to hurry. Without looking out the windshield there was no way to know exactly how much time she had before Caitlyn took the exit off I-75, but it was definitely becoming an issue.

She took a deep breath and let her thoughts wander through the years one last time. Some joyful times, most of them decades earlier, and plenty of sorrow and fear. Then more recently, joy again.

Her eyes began to water and she closed off her mind. Steeled herself for what was to come. And then did what she had to do.

44

C ait glanced from her mother's arm to her face and back again.
Virginia's arm was snaking along the passenger-side door's armrest as her eyes continued to bore resolutely into the closed glove box like it was the most fascinating thing she had ever seen.

She opened her mouth to ask what was going on, and the blast of an air horn from an eighteen-wheel behemoth snapped her attention back to the road. She had started drifting again and damned near sideswiped the truck.

"Dammit," she muttered in frustration and confusion and fear, whipping the wheel to the right. The question she had been about to ask was forgotten.

45

If he could have managed it, Milo would have laughed out loud. The Evil Bitch and Mommy Dearest seemed to be self-destructing right before his borrowed eyes. Connelly was weaving down the highway like a drunken sailor home on leave, while the old biddy seemed to have gone catatonic. Her gaze hadn't lifted from the dashboard in what felt like hours.

What the attraction of the goddamn dashboard was for her, Milo had no clue. She had been staring at it with the unwavering intensity of a religious fanatic. But then, it really didn't matter. The pleasure he was getting from driving the two people he hated so much nearly to the breaking point was something he would relish forever.

The truck blasted its horn and Connelly swerved and cursed and Mommy Dearest did her best impersonation of a catatonic Jack Nicholson in *One Flew Over the Cuckoo's Nest* and Milo thought this might just be one of the best days ever.

He hadn't had this much fun in ages.

46

Virginia's next move was utterly unexpected.

Cait had no sooner gotten the car under control—again—than she turned back to her mother, trying to remember what they had been talking about just before their latest near-wreck. Her nerves were shot and she felt as though she might throw up or have a heart attack at any moment. She didn't know how much longer she could take the stress. She wondered for a split second how long *anyone* could be expected to handle the relentless pressure of Milo Cain without cracking up.

And then she forgot all about it, staring in open-mouthed horror as Virginia Ayers clawed at the door handle.

Missed it.

Clawed at it again and this time her grasping fingers made contact, curling around the metal handle and yanking hard.

Instantly, warm Florida Gulf Coast air began to swirl through the little vehicle, buffeting it as the seventy-mile-per-hour air outside the car tried to force its way inside and equalize the pressure.

Cait's brain vapor-locked. Her mother's actions were so unexpected, so beyond the realm of normal activity that she simply froze, like a computer getting stuck while trying to boot up.

Virginia struggled against the door, her frail body leaning into it and shoving it open against the tremendous force of the air rushing along the outside of a car traveling at highway speeds.

Cait's foot reached instinctively for the brake and she tried to swerve right, into the breakdown lane, but she wasn't next to the breakdown lane, and she nearly sideswiped the same truck they had almost hit just moments ago.

By now, Virginia had managed to open her door maybe two feet. The roar of the big eighteen-wheeler's engine filled Cait's little car and the sound of the pavement rushing beneath them was like water rushing over Niagara Falls, loud and insistent and eternal.

Virginia glanced over at Cait for a split second, and that glance told Cait everything. In her mother's eyes she saw love and regret and sorrow and the unspoken promise that they would meet again someday.

The one thing absent from that hurried glance was fear.

Virginia was unafraid as she looked across the front seat at her only daughter.

Then she shoved the door open fully and tumbled out onto the highway.

47

It all happened so fast Milo had no time to react.

One second he was cackling madly inside his own mind at the effect he was having on Mommy Dearest and The Evil Bitch, forcing them into two near collisions in the span of just a few minutes.

The next second, everything went to shit. Without warning, a blast of tropical air came out of nowhere and highway noise was *right there* and a truck's air horn blew almost right into the old biddy's ear and if Milo had had a physical presence, his body would have been knocked flat on its ass.

The old bitch leaned forward, still staring at the goddamned dashboard, a sight Milo would be happy if he never saw again, and then she looked across the front of the small car at The Evil Bitch, and the moment she did, Milo could feel his hatred begin to build, the unreasoning, unstoppable fury he felt instinctively every time he saw or even thought about Caitlyn Connelly, his despised twin sister.

And then Mommy Dearest looked away and began pushing her ancient body to the right, leaning into the onrushing wind, and then Milo knew what was happening, and he tried to gather his wits and jump into Caitlyn's head before it was too late, and he knew he had to hurry because he only had a second to react, maybe even less, but he had never jumped so quickly and without warning before—even when he was being suffocated earlier today, he had had a *few* moments to prepare—and then the old biddy launched herself out the door.

It happened simultaneously in the blink of an eye and in slow motion. Milo watched, horrified, through his mother's eyes as her body flew out Cait's car and onto the surface of the highway. She forced her eyes to remain open, and Milo knew it was for his benefit, so he could see everything and understand that he had been beaten.

The pavement rushed up to meet them and Virginia's head struck the tar and her body tumbled and the last thing Milo saw was a split-second view of the Florida sky, bright and blue and crystal clear.

48

Cait screamed and slammed on the brakes and barely noticed as her car was rear-ended by a dusty black Lincoln Continental. Her disbelieving eyes were glued to the rearview mirror and she knew she would relive this moment in nightmares for the rest of her life.

Virginia's body struck the pavement and bounced once, limp as a rag doll, somehow avoiding being crushed by the eighteen-wheeler thundering along next to Cait's car. Then it bounced again and rolled into the adjoining travel lane and disappeared beneath the massive frame of another tractor-trailer that had been roaring along behind the first in a mini-convoy.

The truck driver locked up his brakes and black smoke instantly began billowing from beneath his tires, and his trailer threatened to jackknife but he kept it under control until *he* was rammed from behind by another motorist.

Then there was chaos.

Squealing tires mixed with crumpling sheet metal, which mixed with shattering safety glass and the sound of steam hissing from damaged radiators, and all of it came together in a discordant symphony that faded away into the background, overwhelmed inside Cait's head by the sound of her own screams.

She couldn't stop screaming.

She knew she would never stop screaming again.

49

"You look good," Cait said quietly, almost shyly, as she gazed through the wire-reinforced glass of the visiting area at Tampa's Hillsborough County Jail into Kevin Dalton's face. It was a lie, but not *too* much of a lie.

He was pale and had lost weight, but Cait supposed that wasn't surprising under the circumstances. He could make the same observation about her if he chose to, but she knew he would be too kind-hearted to do so.

"I told you to stay away from me," Kevin said quietly, refusing to meet her gaze. "Anything could happen and I don't want you to get hurt." He closed his eyes and rubbed a hand across his haggard face. "I don't want *anyone* else to get hurt, but especially not you."

"It's all over. No one's going to get hurt ever again, at least not by Milo."

Now he did look at her. He did it hesitantly, like he had to work up the courage, but he did it. And when he finally looked into her eyes, he didn't look away. "What do you mean? What happened? Is everyone all right?"

Cait wasn't sure where to start, so she just began talking. She held the plastic telephone handset up to her face and told Kevin everything, and when she got to the part about Virginia sacrificing herself to save Caitlyn, she was proud that she made it halfway through the narrative before breaking down in tears.

Kevin listened without speaking, his face at first impassive but then becoming more and more emotional, until he was crying freely on the other side of the glass, tears rolling down his face in what Cait assumed was probably a mirror image of her own.

When she had finished the story, visiting hours were almost over. All the other visitors had departed and it was just Cait and Kevin and a bored-looking middle-aged guard, standing off by himself in the corner of the room. For a long time no one spoke, and then Kevin said, "How can you be sure he's gone? I mean, really and truly sure?"

Cait shrugged. She had given this question plenty of thought herself over the past two weeks. "I suppose there's no way to be one hundred percent positive, but Milo never demonstrated the ability to jump into anyone's head besides my mother's or mine. I wondered from the moment I picked her up in Sarasota why she was acting so strangely and now I know it's because she was desperate not to tip Milo off to what she was planning and give him the chance to jump into my head. The sensation of pressure never came, so I can only assume she succeeded."

Kevin sat back in an ancient wooden chair and wrinkled his forehead in concentration. "So it's really all over, except it's not over. Milo still wins. I attacked you, and then I attacked an innocent man—my own attorney, no less—in front of a judge in open court. No one's going to believe I wasn't in control of my actions, and even if they did, all that would happen is I'd be committed to a pscyh ward indefinitely. Who knows how long I'm going to be locked up for?"

"I'm going to get you the best representation. I have some money saved up, for a down payment on a house, and now I don't care about a house. I'm going to use every last penny of it to defend you if need be."

Kevin was shaking his head. "No," he said. "Forget me and move on. You're young, accomplished and beautiful. I'll likely be old and beaten-down by the time I get out of here, and then when I do, I'll have no job and no prospects. I certainly can't be a cop anymore. You deserve better. Find someone who can make you happy and settle down."

"I already did," she said quietly.

They stared at each other through the dirty glass, each lost in their own thoughts. After a while, the lights blinked off and on, and the bored, middle-aged guard ambled over. "It's time to go," he said.

Cait nodded and turned back to Kevin. "I'll be back tomorrow, and the day after, and the day after that. We're going to get through this, you'll see."

She placed the handset down in its cradle without waiting for a response. She stood and smiled at Kevin, alone on the other side of the glass. He was still seated in his chair, not in any hurry to leave. There was no reason to hurry because there was nowhere to go.

Cait waited for him to return her smile and after a moment he did. It was hesitant and tremulous, but it was a smile all the same.

It was a start.

Then she turned and walked away.

To be the first to learn about new releases, and for the opportunity to win free ebooks, signed copies of print books, and other swag, take a moment to sign up for Allan Leverone's email newsletter at Allan-Leverone.com.

Reader reviews are hugely important to authors looking to set their work apart from the competition. If you have a moment to spare, please consider taking a moment to leave a brief, honest review of *After Midnight* at your point of purchase, at Goodreads, or at your favorite review site, and thank you.

About the author

A llan Leverone is the *New York Times* and *USA Today* bestselling author of nearly twenty novels, as well as a 2012 Derringer Award winner for excellence in short mystery fiction and a 2011 Pushcart Prize nominee. He lives in Londonderry, New Hampshire with his wife Sue, and has three grown children and two beautiful grandchildren. He loves to hear from readers and other authors; connect on Facebook, Twitter @AllanLeverone, and at AllanLeverone.com

Also by Allan Leverone
Dark Fiction

Mr. Midnight
The Lupin Project
Paskagankee
Revenant
Wellspring
Grimoire
Covenant
Linger: Mark of the Beast (Co-written with Edward Fallon)

Thrillers

The Lonely Mile
Final Vector
Parallax View: A Tracie Tanner Thriller
All Enemies: A Tracie Tanner Thriller
The Omega Connection: A Tracie Tanner Thriller
The Hitler Deception: A Tracie Tanner Thriller
The Kremlyov Infection: A Tracie Tanner Thriller
The Organization: A Jack Sheridan Pulp Thriller
Trigger Warning: A Jack Sheridan Pulp Thriller

Novellas

The Becoming
Flight 12: A Kristin Cunningham Thriller

Story Collections

Postcards from the Apocalypse
Letters from the Asylum
Uncle Brick and the Four Novelettes
The Tracie Tanner Collection: Three Complete Thriller Novels